D1540140

by Laura Chester:

Tiny Talk (1972)
The All Night Salt Lick (1972)
Nightlatch (1974)
Primagravida (1975)
Chunk Off & Float (1978)
Watermark (1978)
Proud & Ashamed (1978)
My Pleasure (1980)
Lupus Novice (1987)
Free Rein (1988)
In the Zone: New and Selected Writing (1988)
The Stone Baby (1989)
Bitches Ride Alone (1991)

Editor:

Rising Tides, 20th Century American Women Poets (1973)
Deep Down, New Sensual Writing by Women (1988)
Cradle and All, Women Writers on Pregnancy and Birth
        (1989)
The Unmade Bed of Married Love (1992)

LAURA CHESTER

Bitches RIDE ALONE

BLACK SPARROW PRESS
SANTA ROSA · 1991

ACKNOWLEDGMENTS

Some of these stories were previously published in *The Berkshire Eagle, Caprice, Revolt in Style, Word of Mouth, Volume Two: Short-short Stories by Women,* and *The Unmade Bed of Married Love.*

Black Sparrow Press books are printed on acid-free paper.

LIBRARY OF CONGRESS CATALOGING-IN-PUBLICATION DATA

Chester, Laura.
    Bitches ride alone / Laura Chester.
        p.   cm.
    ISBN 0-87685-848-5 (cloth)   :   — ISBN 0-87685-849-3 (signed cloth)   :
    —   ISBN 0-87685-847-7 (paper)   :
    I. Title.
    PS3553.H43B58   1991
    813'.54 — dc20   91-31699
                                                                                  CIP

for Tom Moore

CONTENTS

PART III

BITCHES RIDE ALONE

PART ONE

FIRST BASE BOYFRIEND

Is it possible to *know* the first boyfriend, I mean, thirty years later go home again, unfold the first "I love you" note, written on a one-inch piece of paper and made into a tiny bird?

I danced upstairs in my beaver board bedroom, painted pink. I had the whole third floor to myself. Moved up there to get away from my brother, Mister (alias) Davy Crockett. I wanted to sleep alone, listen to Motown and play with my horse collection, in peace. But now I had this other passion.

We had left the lake for the summer, and were back in town. I'd dragged along a wooden sawhorse to ride in front of National Velvet, leaning forward with reins to *leap* into the black and white television.

No one bothered me up there on the third floor. My windows were crowded with ivy. Its minuscule paws seemed to eat right into the red brick of the house. My pink bedroom throbbed with late summer heat, and I could feel the presence of all those *National Geographics,* neatly stacked in the attic beside my room, feel the bare breast-tips of jungle women, as I swivelled on the stool before my vanity and thought about my first boyfriend, the bad boy on the lake.

I had actually met him a couple of years before when I was just a child. I was running water from the big house down the sidewalk to the lake front, and he joined in, though I was in charge. When you turned on the faucet, a wet-lipped river began pushing down the grey cement, breaking new ground, and I was above there, watching, guiding, as the water dipped into a groove or flipped over an edge—a lot like the forming of a life as I see it now—you create this path once and then the river just continues.

That boy, indeed, was on the lip of my experience, beneath the catalpa, dropping orchid boats. We were ten years old, both second-born, and at the mercy of our older brothers. *Ba-by I won-der. Dar-lin' I won-der. Is there An-y-thing that I can Do-ooo-ooo* . . .

I have a photograph of myself at that age, wearing a sleeveless daisy dress, and certain radiance — the pure golden smile of a winner, having guessed the exact number of flashbulbs in the big plastic box during Maxwell Street Days, 114, for this portrait.

My boyfriend and I took refuge in each other and the playhouse down by the water, imitating adult ways with our little brooms and bickering, draining the magic cup of its red-red liquid, only to watch it fill again. I collapsed on the horsehair mattress with its two-foot headboard and appropriate pillows. Wonderful to feel the dimensions fit your body as a child. Then sitting in the small wicker armchairs, a diminutive husband and wife, I'd say, "Do you want to play murder, fire or divorce?"

A couple years later he was lying on top of me, but still we only kissed. He was long like I was, but with lots of auburn hair. I had the golden-green eyes of an animal.

When I laid eyes on him the summer of the love note, I swear I saw him different. He and his brother had a Boston Whaler, and they were attracted by all the commotion from our place. We called it a camp without counselors, but it was a zoo without walls. We had every kind of animal you could think of — llamas, a goat, pigs, peacocks and horses, a pet crow that would land in your hair, and a spider monkey that liked to swing on the telephone wire outside the dining room window. There were also lots of long-legged, blond-headed Amazon girls, aching to get pushed in. Later I wondered what he meant by "wet dream." He had this adult vocabulary.

His family came from a suburb north of Chicago, and he and his older brother, Donny, drove to the country with their Grampa Witt. Donny and my older brother, David

Jerome, also had a friend named Degan, who was rude, very funny, fat and half-French. He spoke with his hands as if everything he saw were an outrage — "She was *bovine,* my dear, perfectly *bovine.*"

They called themselves "The 3 D's," like three blind mice teasing the two of us, because we had leapt beyond them somehow and were feeling that love swarm moving through our bodies as if searching for the proper limb. I sensed it buzzing all about me, just as his boat might circle mine, around and around, being twenty horsepower instead of five.

Degan could imitate all the adults, including "Mean Mona," and "Fat Steve," but his specialty was the "Dreadful Duo," hurling insults and glasses at the latest country club bash, big Don in his madras — "Listen bitch, I want you *in* that car!" Imagine him grabbing her gown by the bosom, her flinging a tray of horse chestnuts wrapped in bacon strips. My boyfriend was sometimes held hostage, and couldn't go out, his father said, till his mother calmed down, which made her all the more furious.

The country was his escape, and Grampa Witt played the harmonica for us, and had this wonderful head of white hair. He said if I were only sixty years older, he'd make me his bride and eat okra soup with me. "Yuk," I'd say, though he was my favorite, like schaum torte, while my boyfriend ordered grasshopper pie — "How can you eat that?" It reminded me of disgusting green shaving cream.

We went on like this, summer after summer, growing more and more aware of each other, though I still was naive, and didn't recognize the smell as I stood to the entrance of his upstairs bedroom, flies dopey on the heated-up windowsill. He grabbed his trunks, then brushed his hand across the bottom silk stripes to my two-piece, sending a shock up in me, like some golden spike — the merging of the rails to be completed.

Then my boyfriend was sent away to boarding school, and we not only promised, we wrote. I saved his letters in the long slender drawers, disguised as columns on either side of my desk. My mother just happened to find them. One had filthy language, and she made my father call a conference. I was not to hear from him again.

Their intuitions were only confirmed when he got kicked out for smoking, and was sent to that school in Switzerland. He got into trouble there too, but returned speaking perfect French. My parents were afraid he would knock me up. *"Au contraire,"* he said, for he was saving me.

But that boy was wild as far as she was concerned, driving his grandfather's Chris Craft like that. Didn't he know other people lived on this lake who wouldn't tolerate that kind of recklessness?

He went full speed ahead—did a complete 360, "Royal Splush," sending out a giant tidal wave. He drove that boat up to Degan's pier one night, and pushed the lever—forward. The engine dug into the water and shoved the entire pier over. The next morning Degan's mother descended: "Ve must have had a te*rrr*ible storme!"

My boyfriend had a sterling silver lighter with his own initials on the side. He told me what it meant to blow smoke in someone's face, and then did it. The nicotine feeling sank down in me, made me dizzy as those drunken flies, wanting to try out the twin-sized bed in his boyhood room, but something inside me said not to. *Don't* unpeel that golden coin, your currency, it's such a thin wafer to dissolve in your mouth or stuck on the roof with port wine, the body and blood of my boyfriend, there on my knees untasted.

He told me how he loved the little groove that travelled from my breastbone down to my belly, how hard and sexy my stomach was, and that made me a little reticent, though I did let him run a finger up and down this tight demarcation between the two more dangerous places.

He never got beyond first base, though he went all-the-way with some Chicago girl out in the tea house of their rose garden. He always said he respected me, though I kept him playing pickle for a while, and even if I liked lying down behind the pump house in my Bermuda shorts and having him lie between my legs, I kept my arm guarding my AA breast and he only got more excited. *Feels like Fire, burnin' in my soul, FIRE Fire, burnin' in my soul.*

We'd stumble up, ruffled and damp, off to take a fast drive to The Kiltie, fresh to the yellow line and punches on the radio, playing "Major Lance" and *Baby love, my Baby love . . .* "Stop this car!" We'd jump out on the small town street, run around and *whoop* until the light turned green — then off to order suicide sundaes, caramel as well as fudge, with Alley Oop crankin' and The Doors — lighting sweet Old Golds, blowing smoke rings, sunburn still exciting our skin — then the ripe smell of cornfields along Sawyer Road driving home, whole families of raccoon trotting into them.

I broke his boarding school heart that year and stopped writing over the winter. I was going out with Cricker Costigan of football fame, but the varsity year was soon over. *My boyfriend's back and there's gonna be trouble — Hey nonny Nah, my boyfriend's back . . .*

So there we were when summer came around, going to the drive-in movies. I was in the front seat with this new guy, who kept picking at the cuff to my hot pants, my real boyfriend fixed-up in back. I kept turning around to talk, until sudden anger seized me — seeing him in the rearview mirror, kissing that little townie!

We started in again, as if we just couldn't quit, though he was getting more sophisticated, and said things like "Chemistry," meaning what went on, and "You taste so familiar, *mmm.* Want a drag?" He said he really liked my smell. It had something to do with the heat of horses, cocoa butter and the mud smell of algae down my bathing suit. He sometimes used an aftershave, Bay Rum, and I'd smooth a little on my arm, rub my lips and face all over the anisette likeness as if I really wanted deep trouble.

Then I went off to college and didn't wait. I was the first of my friends to get married.

After the birth of my son, my boyfriend arrived with a silver rattle. He was wearing the first digital watch I'd ever seen, and was much taller than my husband. I was struck by his Continental good looks — articulate, thin, with a real reputation. He indicated that I'd ruined him, said something about Love being a good excuse for always fucking up. He had always shocked and excited me, even when I didn't know what he was talking about.

Now his chest looked smooth, impossibly tan and untouchable. We were both twenty-five and I was nursing a baby, and he was still shooting a rooster tail spray of water up from his single ski. I threw the towel over my baby's head and laughed as he drenched me completely. I knew he wanted a better look at my bathing suit top, half down, breasts much bigger with the milk in.

He came and sat down beside me at the end of the pier, sat close enough to let his leg rest against mine, and it felt cool from the water, as mine was hot from the sun. *But like a honeybee's sting, you gone and left my heart in pain . . .* The baby was sleeping under the beach towel in my arms, while we sat and talked quietly, remembering things, talking like we'd always done, perfectly content, yet almost without content, that summer day spilling with history into the present moment.

I was touched by the gift for my baby, who would batter it with his healthy hammering. I would save the rattle and many years later, mail it back to him when his daughter was born. Perhaps she'd grow up to fall in love with my boy, bringing us all full circle.

I was just my son's age when my boyfriend gave me his ID bracelet. The top part opened and I kept his photo inside. He was wearing a black and red wool checked jacket, and his name was inscribed across the top.

When I separated from my husband at the age of thirty-five my boyfriend was the first man I contacted. He lived in Boston now and was a landscape architect. I didn't explain my present situation, because I knew he was married and didn't want him to think I was seeking him out for anything. He didn't tell me that his wife had moved out. He just said that she was staying at their place on The Cape. We had dinner alone, and he wore a pale green cotton sweater that made his darkness even more disarming. He ordered the best Japanese food I'd ever tasted, and we drank too much sake and talked all night, laughing loudly over horrible things — how Douglas Schmidt had burned their summer house down, on purpose, with his mother inside it — "What a freak!"

"You know our spider monkey got electrocuted," I told him, "swinging on a live wire outside the big house. And Degan was in a terrible boat accident — the propeller nearly chewed him up. If it hadn't been for Carey Sledge stripping off the top to her two-piece and jumping in to tie a tourniquet, he'd be belly up right now."

"What a sight that must have been," he added, for she was quite a dish. We were both surprised that she could think so fast.

I was genuinely sorry about his brother, who'd been committed to a mental institution. His roommate had smashed him over the head with a guitar, and now my boyfriend was the only heir.

He admitted that he was seeing a therapist twice a week, and she was too. Plus, they were seeing a counselor together. He said how they got into these fights, not unlike his father and mother. *Bombs Away!*

For some reason he had never used his temper on me, though I knew it was there like a bag of M-80's, and could picture his marriage as explosive — how they drank too much and fought and fucked, with passion, but not compassion.

"Maybe we have to change our definition of love," I said, as we strolled together after dinner, arm in arm. I was personally tired of tension and anxiety, and it seemed as if we should graduate into a new kind of amorous ease, lulling as the shoreline wave lap.

"Do you remember when Donny climbed on top of me," I asked him. "Right before he was committed, down on the pier? He said how he had to have me, and it was like some big joke that was getting out of hand until you and my brother pulled him off of me?"

I'd been disturbed by that, but mainly felt sorry, for he was so terribly awkward and no girl loved him, no one wrote his name on the edge of her books, or signed off — *Je t'embrasse fort*. I remember my boyfriend writing that someday we'd marry, and that seemed unlikely. Where did all that correspondence go?

"M.M. probably burned it," he laughed. He always hightailed it when he saw her coming. She would swoop on our love and scare the golden bird away. He knew when to move. But he'd be back again — I could always count on that.

Love is often like a visitation, isn't it? Even when it reappears. Like this afternoon, I'm wondering, because I've got this lush anticipation of something sweet returning, *Are you ready for a brand new beat? Summer's here and the time is right, for dancin' in the street.*

Thirty years later, and it seems a little strange, but I bet he'd still taste familiar, and we would pick right up, finding the proper grip, and start batting balls back and forth.

He used to throw his tennis racket over the morning-glory fence, and was reported to have shot his BB gun at fishermen. I encouraged his wildness, being a quiet rebel myself, a bit of a bad girl with a puella shine. He resented the fact that people expected a performance, still, at the age of forty.

Once I made him a birthday survival kit, with everything

he needed, including Beeman's gum and Marlboros, a replica of the baby-blue Mustang he drove, a rubber — which I thought quite risqué, a tiny bottle of vodka and playing cards for poker, a purple rabbit's foot key chain with the key to my heart, and a Playboy Bunny insignia.

We used to look at those magazines together, and I also found that smooth burst of skin quite exciting, and could see why guys had to have it. He was kind to me anyway, saying — "Hey, don't worry, more than a handful is wasted."

While he was married, I always wrote to both of them. If I sent an invitation, it was always to them both, but still she was jealous, and he went out of his way to convince her I was just a childhood friend, mere puppy love, that's all. I didn't like him belittling what we'd had, even if jealousy weren't called for. I never did meet her, because she wouldn't show up, and then we would dance off together. *Sugar Pie Honey Bunch, you know that I weep for you, I can't help myself, I love you and nobody else, doom doom, doom-doom . . .*

Their final separation agreement was signed the day before the birth of their daughter. He wasn't allowed to go to the hospital, and I drove into Boston to be with him, sleeping on the sofa bed. I could see that he was in pain. It came up in his throat and then stayed there with a vile and burning sensation. He couldn't seem to get away from it.

I wanted to lead him back into memory, back to the cool, dark places of our childhood, back down those slippery steps into the lower level of the boat house, where we leaned into the damp smell of mud-filled shells and boat bottom slime, rotten life preservers stuck in the salamander room, where we'd go and light matches, the air so dense, it seemed like a gas that might explode.

I wanted to sit in the drier darkness of the abandoned squash court, secretly, one to one, hiding out, barely kissing, lips innocent unto lips — then to rush back into the shock of daylight, leap into our boats and race across the lake, the

21

batting rhythm of the bows slapping water, feet flat on the vibrating plexiglas, how nothing seemed to matter other than the great indivisibles of sun, water, love and lake air.

And now he was driving across the state to come see me. I changed the sheets on the guest bed and made grilled salmon for dinner. I knew he would come prepared, armed with tennis racket and hiking boots, the kind of man who would arrive bringing five house presents, including a pot of spectacular cyclamen.

It had been a hard summer, I could hear it in his voice, and I wanted to open my arms to him, encompass him with light, like that girl in the photo, take him back and myself back there with him, safe into the underbrush.

We used to pull his boat up on our own secret island, way back through that squish of lily pads and seaweed, running the engine in reverse to clear the propeller, hiding from the belligerence of brothers.

Sometimes Degan threw a stick of dynamite into the canal sending a spray of gunk over my boyfriend and me. We tossed water balloons from the bridge in revenge, bombing Donny and Dave, with those rubbery boobs, a surprise attack — *poom poom.*

The lake is the same now, only older. When we were growing up, the lake seemed to be living out its adolescence. Everyone had a ton of kids, and boats zoomed around with water skiers, sailfish were pulled behind outboard motors, a gush of water shooting up the centerboard slot, and cub boats turned together — *comin'aroun'port,* fireworks bursting over bobbing observers.

When Grampa Witt finally died at the age of a hundred, the family promptly sold his summer property, and now many people have built homes all along the point, and the lake has settled into middle age.

Still, I think back to that beach grass out there, dividing the main lake from the bay, how the trees eased up and the sun felt softer, how boats had to drive far off-shore, because of the sandbars going through the channel, securing our love nest with privacy.

Now he was the kind of man who built these wonderful gardens, who loved the subtle pink smell of phlox, the sticky green smell from the stalks of cleome, his arms strong from pruning and digging, earth ground into his fingertips. He admitted that his wife always disliked his gardening, because her father ran a working greenhouse. She wanted her own set of golf clubs.

Now neither of us was married for the first time, since—
Stop, in the name of love, before you break my heart, Think it Oh oh-ver, Ooo-ooo. Think it Oh oh-ver.

I think about how we used to ask questions of that Magic 8 Ball—twice it said, "Definitely yes." I was stuffing my mouth with Teaberry gum, wanting to chew all five pieces. How could anyone so oral not kiss with her tongue? But he was never one to push me.

Like that night I spent in his apartment—it was fine that I chose to sleep on the sofa bed. The next morning we had a leisurely breakfast, unlike most city dwellers, who never have time. We were both cleaning up, when a friend of his arrived, and joking he put his hands on my shoulders, said—"Meet the new wife," and I laughed, saying—"Not so fast!"

And how we'd probably be having homemade waffles at my house with real maple syrup and mango tea, when some guy would call up and I'd reach behind me for the wall phone, say—"Hi, guess what? I'm having breakfast with my *first* boyfriend," who would have to correct me, saying—"First and *last,*" and I would have to repeat that, feeling like we were still playing house, only this time—it was All the way home.

IF YOU GOT IT SO TOGETHER
WHAT'S THAT ALL AROUND YOU

For some reason when my horse stepped on my foot the other day and crushed my little toe, I thought about the time I found my older brother, Jerome, in bed with Amanda Benson.

I can't explain why I put these two things together. I don't think the discovery of my brother hurt as much as the horse did. It didn't hurt so much as it made me furious. I was mad for several reasons, the first being—I hate to be lied to. I was also tired, and last but not least—I was not in love. Neither was my brother, and that's what made me angry. Or maybe disgusted is a better word.

This carnal event took place in my grandmother's summer home on Oconomowoc Lake. It wasn't summertime, that's for sure. It was very late fall, probably November and already freezing. No one used the big house in winter, except for the occasional ice boating party when the place was opened up.

Closing the house in September meant putting a large white sheet over every piece of furniture, including the grand piano. I thought this ritual had little to do with reality. Was dust really going to fall as thick as snow and ruin the upholstery? It was more a way of putting the place to sleep, sort of like a funeral service, and my brother walked into this furniture graveyard and allowed me to wake the dead.

We'd been over at a party at Rowboat Shraeder's, who lived on a rival lake. Rowboat was one year older than me and a year younger than my brother, otherwise my brother and I didn't socialize, being two years apart.

Rowboat's father had been amusing himself in the role of chaperone by spitting 100 proof alcohol up into the air and setting it on fire. I thought this pretty strange behavior, and that things were getting out of hand.

I can't remember who my date was that night, and I for one didn't drink much. I forget why I had to locate my brother. Were we sharing a car? That seems unlikely, but I don't want to just make up what's no longer clear to me. The rest of the picture's too memorable.

Anyway, Jerome decided to have an after-party at my grandmother's house, and a bunch of them were dropped off there. My date must have been a junior, because he drove me over. Douglas and Degan and another couple were there in the living room, sitting on the white draped furniture, drinking something out of a silver pocket flask and looking bored stiff, or perhaps, half-frozen, for even though the fire was roaring away, it was having little effect.

I like to eat my fruit in season, and something about this scene made me think of some cheap fruit cocktail with the acid taste of tin. "Where's Jerome?" I demanded.

"We couldn't find him," Degan said, and I thought — What an ignoramus. Had he spooked from room to room with a white sheet over his head, mewling about for my brother? Perhaps he'd been afraid of the dark upstairs. It was a pretty big house.

"What do you mean you couldn't *find* him."

"We looked all around," he protested. But I smelled my brother's cigar. He thought he was Mr. Big sometimes, God's gift. But I wasn't in the mood for this and Gramma would die if she saw.

"Well I'll go find him if you can't," I said. It was a quarter to one and I had a curfew. Did Amanda Benson, my classmate, know what the hell she was doing? She was the slinkiest girl in my tenth grade class, with sleek black hair and these juju-bee lips. She seemed to know something the rest of us didn't. Maybe that's why we all ganged up on her.

I marched up those stairs, where I'd played pick-a-hand

with my cousins half a decade ago, hiding an acorn in one fist, descending or mounting, depending.

Maybe my brother and Amanda had passed out on the bathroom floor. My grandparents had this huge Oriental style bathroom with lots of mirrors and black tile, but no one was taking a shower. No one was in the master bedroom either with its formal lacquered furniture.

I went through the blue and then the rose guest rooms, my aunt and uncle's quarters, their kids bedrooms, one, two, and three, down to the end of the hallway, all the way to Vernon's room. He was my favorite boy cousin. We were born on the exact same day.

It felt chilly upstairs, no love nest here, just a leftover smell of summer gone stale, of cardboard coming from the stack of board games on top of his dresser. Parcheesi was my favorite, with those little wooden men in bright colors, the mathematical balance of the four-part design. My brother, Jerome, always made blockades. It was the only way he knew to win.

"Jerome," I called out, but nobody answered, not a sound. And what about my date now I wonder. Was he looking like another stiff downstairs with his hands stuffed into his pockets? Who the fuck was he? Certainly nobody I wanted to drag upstairs. No one I would even kiss. "Jerome!" I gave up. "Come out." Did he expect me to count to three hundred?

Finally I thought of Goetschie's room, through that side door, down another hallway, on the way to the back stairs, which descended to the kitchen. She had been my father's nanny, and had taken care of all four children in his family growing up. She was like the white cloth over motherhood, keeping the fabric fine, Miss Goetsch, though we always called her Goetschie.

I swung into her bedroom and needed no light, for the smell was obviously different. It was like some squished and heated up overripe fruit at the bottom of a summer trash can. The light from the front porch illuminated all I wished I'd never seen — Amanda Benson roiling around on top of my brother who was lying bare-chested beneath her. I saw the satin shine of the comforter slide from her shoulders, and said, "I think it's time to go." Then I fled down the hallway feeling all askew from a pain I couldn't get away from, for the primal scene had arrived quite late and stomped its impression on my memory.

But how dare those jerks send me up there into this? I burst down the stairs in a fury. "Thanks!" I said, "I found him, and we're leaving!" They all had the look of plain liars. I flew out the stone floored entranceway, slamming the big front door so hard the entire plate glass panel shattered.

I jumped in the car, jammed the seat back and forth, trying to arrest my own feelings. Within minutes they were ready to roll. At least making a scene gets action. I didn't say a word, didn't turn around to snarl when he brought these words to his defense. "We weren't *doing* anything," he said. "We were just making hot chocolate."

I'm a literal girl, that gullible, but this was too much to believe. I was the kind of sister who kept rolling dice, even when the game was obviously over, but this lie seemed so preposterous, I thought maybe there was some hidden truth.

I didn't turn around to sneer at Amanda Benson, who was happily crammed in with all three of them, while my invisible date and I sat miles apart. She was giggling and making little yum-yum sounds, before my brother lost his lunch out the window. I rolled down my own to get air.

Just a few years before, my brother and I had delighted in buying a fake puddle of barf in this magic shop in Amsterdam. We also bought a plastic turd, but Dad took that and threw it into the canal before mother got a chance to see it. We were allowed to keep the puke patch though, and we were already making plans on where we would place it to really shock Goetschie.

Miss Goetsch was no longer with us, and I wondered if

the dead were judgmental. Did they look down on earth, see who was sliding away there under the slippery satin comforters? I pictured her with hands on hips, enough to stop the hottest orgy. Her ghost would be going out to bang on the big bell, exorcising the nasties from the house.

I glanced in the rear view mirror. Amanda's shirt looked sloppy and her hair all ratted. Somebody groaned that he had to take a leak, and did so to the brim in a Pabst beer bottle. Amanda shrieked and I flashed a killer look at all of them that said, "Grow up."

I didn't say a word to Mom or Dad, but it's amazing what parents don't know. My silence was giving me power. At least Jerome was nice for a couple of days. I had achieved a kind of moral superiority, not knowing that that always eventually backfires.

At least Jerome got Degan to drive him out to the country, and they replaced the pane of heavy glass, and no more was said about it. We were all just lucky the pipes didn't freeze.

But how could I face Amanda Benson now. And we were in the same homeroom. I was too embarrassed to help ruin her reputation which was already pretty far gone.

A couple years later, Amanda was the obvious choice to do the annual strip tease in the Senior Show. It was an all girls' school, and mostly a female audience, but word got out that Amanda Benson certainly knew how to move her hips. I pictured her swivelling motion, and imagined a rotary blender or whisk, and suddenly the thought occurred to me — so *that's* how hot chocolate is made.

THE MOST HANDSOME MAN
WHO EVER LIVED

My friend Christine always wanted to write a story about my brother Jerome and call it, "The Most Handsome Man." I was going to write my own version, closer to the truth, though less objective. While my brother *is* tall, dark and unusually good looking, I have never had a fondness for his stance.

I really thought I should leave this to Christine, until one day crossing 5th Avenue, I saw a man who was even *more* handsome. He was ready to jog into the park. I was wearing this enormous straw hat with silk flowers, the kind of hat that encourages others, but I reeled when he turned this dangerous smile on me and said simply, "You look sad."

I answered that I was just tired, exhausted from a fight with the man I was then seeing. I had a novel under my arm, and he said that he'd written a book on malpractice. I asked him if he knew this other lawyer, as if all lawyers in New York were familiar. He discovered that I lived in the country. He also had a house a half hour away. I said, "How can you run in this weather? Wouldn't you rather go riding?"

"That's funny," he said. "I'll be riding next week in the redwoods." Then he told me his name which was disturbing, for his first name was also Jerome. I glanced off his shoulders, his amazing blue eyes, and wondered if this were an illicit act somehow, having found someone even more handsome, robbing my brother of his glory.

I knew Christine wanted to write about those women who approached my brother with this opener — "Oh my God, I used to date a man who looked just like you!" As if they had ever. How obvious.

But now Jerome had to run in another direction. He had

already gone out of his way. So I went spinning back to the man on West 83rd Street, where I would discover I was indeed sad.

I called Christine who lives on East 91st and said, "I just met the most handsome man. But I can't remember his last name." I had been too distracted by the Jerome part.

Why did Jerome always have to ruin everything. *If you can't say something nasty don't say anything at all.* And where were my parents I'd like to know, when he gave me those snakebites or rubbed knuckles across my scalp. He laughed as if I were a walking punch line. At least I was faster than he was, and he did say proudly, in his own defense, that I would probably go to the Olympics.

When I remembered the name of the little town where the most handsome man lived on weekends, I drove out of my way to look in a phone book. Was it Alberg, or Albers, no, Alger, Jerome Alger. There it was inscribed. The name of the most handsome man in print. The one who had negated my brother.

How thrilled I was, beside myself. I would write this man a postcard, ask him casually about his trip, suggesting a country ride sometime. I sent a picture of two amicable horses, painted by my brother's favorite artist, George Stubbs.

Of course both Jeromes were lawyers, and that also put me on guard. There's a certain hardness that comes from being the first born, protecting some deep disappointment.

When he called I felt instantly winded, though he teased me about corresponding. "Ever think about becoming a writer?"

"Naaa," I laughed, "no money in that!"

He was dating a girl long-distance. She lived in Austin. They spoke every night. She was coming for a visit and he would rent a carriage, take her to the Rainbow Room.

He offered to fix me up with his neighbor. *"Fine,"* I said, a little disappointed. In the country one cultivates patience.

I wrote him another postcard, and thanked him for being so considerate. I sincerely wished him luck—"What more could she possibly want?" I imagined that she was gorgeous, and only rode English. My brother looks great in his outfit when he hunts.

The hounds ran around and around his country place last Christmas, chasing an actual fox. I'm sure he would have loved to have had that on film, but his wife was protecting their daughters from the rampage and couldn't risk running for the camera.

I can't imagine being married to my brother, even if every eye follows him through the airport and his clothes are impeccably dark. When he puts a stack of papers on a table, all voices stop talking. When he stands to make a toast—an eloquence flows.

When Jerome the most handsome finally arrived at my door, I was bowled over. He was even better than I had remembered, wearing a bright flannel shirt that made his eyes quite shocking. He strode in with every bit as much assurance as my brother would have had, wanting to see the whole house. He punched the bag that hung in the basement, and I felt the impact of something from my childhood. I had a hard time looking at him, you know? I had to turn my head away, as if something might break. He had just broken up with his girlfriend.

He couldn't stop talking about it. Betrayal at the deepest level. She'd gotten pregnant by another man. And now he would never have a baby. The conversation over lunch kept repeating like the ringing of some phoney phone call—I had to answer in order to speak to him, knowing he was calling someone else.

It hurt him to think about family, the tromping of his hopefulness. It reminded him of other failures, the arrival of his sister, how he'd never been loved, right from the beginning: *Dear Mom.* "Shove off," my brother had said to her.

I forced myself to look at this stranger and thought, if I were to marry the most handsome of men, and he took my last name, since "Jerome Alger" is a mouthful, then there would be *two* Jerome Faithornes, rivals for the rival position.

My brother's wife is also named Julia. Once at a family wedding, my sister-in-law and I were both dressed in purple. A rather drunken fellow came up to us and asked me my name. "Julia Faithorne," I answered, then he turned to her. "I'm Julia Faithorne also," she said.

I like my sister-in-law. She has to put up with a lot. In some ways I think of her as having saved me from my childhood—how he pushed me into "Spit Sea" which lay between our sleeping porch beds, how he said he'd give me a quarter if I didn't cry all day, then waited till it was almost sunset. My first memory is of being in the tub with him, and then there was this little brown log. Imagine being that familiar, and now he doesn't write or even call.

Jerome invited me to his place the next weekend. We sat on a bench out on the porch to his house. As he spoke I thought he grew younger, and became like a very small boy, and I was just a girl beside him. We were holding hands as the sun went down and the ceiling was a baby blue. He put his arm around me, and his eyes began to fill as he spoke. We kissed very lightly, as children might, and bluebirds sailed around the house.

I dreamt of making love to this man and woke thinking about my brother, how we each had a wrought iron lamp. Mine pictured a girl, running in a skirt, while his was just a walking boy. When my brother moved into another room, I missed counting June bugs on the screen with him, guessing whose car was coming up the drive, how we raced to lower the canvas when a downpour came, how we survived our various housekeepers.

I remember him dialing the police on the disconnected wall phone, because Angeline was trying to poison us, making us eat raspberries crawling with little worms. I remember him throwing cherry bombs down the cistern, then hiding under my bed when the cops came. He called Tip Hawkins almost every night to talk about the Hard Core Six, but he never really dated anyone.

I said to my new friend Jerome, "You might think you're too old at forty-five now, but you look thirty-five and act twenty-five. I bet you probably wish you were still fifteen, but when you get right down to it, Jerome, you know you're only five years old."

"Right," he said, turning me around. "And now I'm going to teach you how to kiss." His weekend beard cut into my skin. How difficult some men are. But how could we live without them?

"Perfectly well," Christine might say, because we do have these full and satisfying lives and I'm thankful every day, for my three equine, two canine, one feline and two fine boys.

Maybe Christine will come visit this summer and I'll introduce her to Jerome. Maybe I'll start wearing his hand-me-downs, bounce on his bed and get into fights with him. He might not be the most handsome man who ever lived, but if we race, I'm going to let him win.

THE ANSWER

He couldn't decide if he should marry. He was already in his 40's and he'd never been married. People said that he'd be the perfect partner except for this flaw. Being a bachelor had become a stigma. But for the last couple of years he'd had this idea that he wanted to get married. He even spoke of it the first time we met, though he wasn't referring specifically to us.

"What do you think you want?" he asked.

I said I'd be happy with a committed weekend relationship. "I'm not saying I'm against marriage. I just don't believe in divorce."

But he thought he wanted a baby. Everybody else had a baby.

"Even if a child were conceived," I said, "we still wouldn't have to get married."

"Not with me, kid." He believed one got married first.

I began to wonder if he only wanted to get married because he thought that he should. Or if he did get married, would he only be trying it on to see how it felt? Maybe he had doubts about me, if I were the right woman.

He admitted to friends that he wasn't sure. One friend admitted to me this admission. That friend said that I should sit him down and ask *him* to get married.

"No way José," I answered.

Still, one night I confronted him. "Do you think we'll ever get married?"

"I don't know," he said.

"What don't you know. If I'm the right one?"

"I don't know," he said.

"Well then why don't you go ask God," I suggested.

He looked at me oddly. He was more likely to ask the cigarette he was smoking.

"Really," I smiled. "Just try it. Go on. Go in the other room and ask."

He got up slowly, then put out the cigarette and left the room.

I sat on the bed, thinking about what God would say to him. I imagined God would say, "Do you think you'll find anyone better? Of course not. So go ahead." I had to believe in that answer.

Suddenly he returned. He was also smiling.

"What did He say?" I asked.

"He said no."

"That's funny." I must have looked disappointed. "That's not what He told me."

"What did He say to you?"

"I guess I didn't really ask," I admitted. "I was only trying to overhear your conversation."

"But," he paused, "I still want to marry you."

I looked at him blankly.

"What do you say?" he asked.

"How can I say yes, if God said no?" I responded.

"He didn't really say No. I just made that up."

"So you didn't really ask?"

"I felt stupid," he admitted.

"That's all right. That's how you're supposed to feel. We *are* stupid."

"*I'm* not," he responded. And then he stood up. I thought he was going to leave. Maybe he had his answer and it was over.

"Where are you going?" I asked.

"In the other room."

"What are you going to do?"

He walked to the door and then looked at me. "I'm going to see if He changed His mind," he said.

THE INTRODUCTION

The first thing his mother said to me was "*You're* not Jewish."
People always took me for Scandinavian, which I wasn't either. "Well I'm part Jewish," I lied.

"Ma, what do you care."

"*I'm* Jewish," she asserted.

"And how many times have you ever been to temple," he asked her. She appeared to think about that.

"Never," she answered, though she apparently cared. She was in a Catholic nursing home. There was a cross on the wall. She didn't like lying there and who could blame her.

"You want these people to know you're not Catholic," I said, sitting down close to the bed.

"Yes," she said. "I'm Jewish."

"So you have two boys," I went on, to put us on equal ground. "I have boys too."

She looked at her son. "I'm healthy," she accused him.

"You have beautiful skin," I told her, and she looked in my eyes and nodded yes. Her skin was very smooth, almost without a wrinkle. Her frail body barely filled half the bed. For a second we seemed in agreement.

It was Passover, and on the way to the nursing home, Mel and I had discussed what "pass over" meant. He said it referred to the Jews passing out of Egypt, but I thought it related to the angel of death passing over. "The lintel of each Jewish household was marked with blood."

"Lentil?" he said.

"So the eldest son would be saved."

"Do you know why we eat matzo at Passover?" he quizzed me.

"Because leaven relates to evil?"

"Because there wasn't time to let the bread rise," he answered. "But I'm not a religious person."

I believed that I was, because I didn't care about our petty differences.

"I'm Jewish," his mother announced. I had been pleased that he wanted me to meet her.

"Practically all my friends are Jewish," I had told him, "but do you think I've ever been invited to a Seder?"

He started telling his mother about his job at *The Christian Science Monitor,* how he was the only Jewish man on the floor. And how weird they were, never smoking or drinking, not going to see doctors — What if you *needed* a doctor. And how they made jokes about Jews.

"I told you," she said. "Didn't I tell you?"

It was like the-brown-and-the-blue-eye club. Mel ate pork and shellfish. You can't be sometimes Kosher. Even Catholics ate meat on Fridays now, and boys were allowed in girls' dorms. Rules change.

"Did you know that the Last Supper was a Seder?" I'd asked him on the car ride out. Yes, he knew that. But did he know on the night of that Seder, Jesus drank from Elijah's cup?

"I'm healthy!" his mother announced.

He looked at me with humored patience, accepting his mother totally. When he described his relationship to her, it reminded me of mine with my eldest son.

"Do you love me as much as you loved Liza?" I asked him.

Instead of answering, he responded, "Well, I don't love you as much as my Mother." I thought that an inappropriate response. I would hardly compare my feelings for him to those for my father.

"I'm healthy," she said out loud.

The nurse came in to feed his mother, and began with dessert, ice cream, instead of the pea soup which followed, a disgusting progression. Two bites and she cried, "I'm full." But the nurse kept prodding her with nourishment.

"That's enough."

"Come on, Ma," he said.

"I'm alive!" she burst out.

"If we could bring you something, anything to eat, what would you like," I asked her.

"Grapes," she said. "Red grapes. I'm full!" But then she accepted another bite. After each bite she said, "That's enough."

His mother was not much older than mine, my mother with her whirlwind energy. I doubted if she'd ever end up in a nursing home. She was more apt to kill herself speeding to church in a car.

"I don't love you anymore," she said to her son. "Get out of here!"

He looked surprised.

"You don't mean that," I said, more shocked than he was. "You're just mad that he's going away on a trip, and you won't see him for a while."

"Yes," she said.

"We're both going to miss him."

"Yes," she said.

The nurse was still aiming mouthfuls, but now his mother turned her head completely away and said her last, "Enough." So the nurse gave up and took away the tray, explaining that they had to force feed her.

His mother had been a fantastic cook. Her son certainly loved to eat. I had never made matzo ball soup, but enjoyed it when it was homemade. I thought gefilte fish were born in a jar. I wanted to have his baby. I doubted if he would ever get married. He was a great lover. I thought he would be a good father too. I let him say good-bye to his mother alone.

I waited down the hall where I couldn't hear their conversation, but could imagine her saying how I already *had* children. "Too old for you. You need a Jewish wife."

When he came out of his mother's room, he looked lovable and sad, sexy and vulnerable, beaten, yet also unbeatable. He looked better than any other man to me. I would do anything for him.

"Well," I said, walking towards him, taking his hand, "what did she say?"

"Nothing," he acted surprised.

"Didn't you ask about me?"

"No," he said.

After my father met Mel I wanted to know — What did he think? And my father had answered, "I liked him *very* much." I'd expected no less, but now I wanted her approval.

"Why didn't you ask?" I wondered. "Don't you care what your own mother thinks?"

"Excuse *me*," he said. But I was also offended, and he hated to see me upset.

"She thought you were pretty and very nice," he went on. "Easy to get to know."

"Why say that? Why lie about it?"

"I doubt if she even knew you were there," he said.

HISSSTORY

It's scary," he said, appalled by the size of his own dick. "Even when I was an infant, my mother used to show me off in Riverside Park."

These mothers of the mid-50's would stroll their babies in perambulators and compare the penises of their tiny sons.

"Your mother must have been very proud," I said.

"It just made the others defensive. *Their* little boys were normal."

His mother had been concerned — How would he fit in?

His father had been threatened by the arrival of the enormous infant cock. All through childhood this father was hard on his son. Men never admit to jealousy.

Girl friends were few, but once in a while there was the rare one who loved him for himself alone. "You have such a sweet personality. I know you'd never hurt me."

But he was afraid his cock might indeed hurt if given its head. Unleashed, he pictured a St. Bernard trying to be a lap dog. Instead of a single scoop cone, he was a gallon of ice cream.

But finally he met Mala, and she was a mere 6' 2". He hoped that she would accommodate him. She was also a virgin.

"Does it scare you?" he asked her that night on the sofa. Woman always love sofas.

"Is it supposed to?" she asked.

"Of course not, but look how big it is."

She touched the head and it jumped. "All my life," she admitted, "people have been pointing out my size. I always found that oppressive."

He couldn't believe she understood. "May I look at you?" he asked her. She shrugged. She didn't see why not, but he drew back in horror. "I couldn't possibly fit in there!"

"Am I smaller than other women?"

"Much!" he screamed.

When she left, he threw himself on the bed, yelled, "FUCK," for he feared he never would.

He grounded his cock that evening. He wouldn't let it out. He made it refrain from drink and dance. He just kept it inside the apartment, until it got as depressed as he was.

But one morning he woke up, reached down and there was nothing there. His dick was gone! He walked into the living room, and saw a note pinned to the sofa. "Write when you get work." It had taken all the money out of his wallet and his best Italian clothes.

His father said, "That penis always was a problem. Not that *I* minded its size, but if you'd only had a normal one, things might have turned out differently."

With his dick gone, his mood became lighter, and he decided to turn his life around.

The woman who interviewed him at the bank seemed highly sympathetic. She told him that they usually only hired enormous penises, while he didn't even have one to interview. Still, she wanted to believe his story, and gave him the job on a trial basis.

That very night, he heard a knock on the door, and when he opened up, he saw another dick outside, standing there on the mat. This one had a message in an envelope, "I traded places with my cousin, Manu. Thought you might be more happy with him. Anyway, give him a go. I'm having a great time in Kenya."

What was odd, was that this dick was black, and he was white, but it seemed to be a perfect fit. It certainly pleased the lady at the bank, who admitted that the board had been hoping to hire a black dick for years, and they would be pleased to meet a nice average one that could also walk like a white man.

She gave his adorable, normal size penis a magnificent contract, and he gave her a ring in exchange. She was the perfect partner, wife and mother, in business and in bed. She loved his adopted black penis as if it were their very own.

His father became agreeable, took back his proper position as head of the family, allowing his son to grow up. Their only fear was that the original dick might tire of travel, and someday return to take its rightful place and ruin their lives forever.

HIS SWEATER

I first noticed the sweater on the upper shelf of his closet that night when I couldn't sleep. I didn't want to disturb him, so I tried lying on the sofa, but felt chilled alone. That's when I found the sweater, a rosy shade of grey, luscious yarn with flicks of angora woven into it. Not a masculine sweater, I thought, but it got me through the night.

I remember with fondness the anxiety in his voice, calling my name the next morning. He brought me back into his big bed and I believe we even made love again. He seemed to like seeing his sweater on me.

As the weekend continued I asked if I could borrow it while he was gone.

At first he said, no, that he thought he'd take it with him.

"To the desert?" I asked.

He thought so.

But on the day before departure he mentioned, "Didn't you say something about borrowing that sweater?"

My heart seemed to suddenly open.

"But don't wear it every day," he warned.

Once he was gone, I wore it more than occasionally. I even slept with it sometimes, but as the weeks went by, I noticed the arms of the sweater grew longer, and I had to roll up the cuffs. The once tight middle now lapsed into a loosened sag. I imagined it good for pregnancy.

One night I was wearing it while knitting up a sweater for the unborn baby of a friend, when the phone rang. I knew it was him, calling from Cairo. Sometimes I *know* these things.

He worried about his sweater long distance. It was worth four hundred and fifty dollars, he said, designed by the mother of an old girlfriend.

I realized I should never have borrowed it. I sensed he regretted his moment of generosity.

Days later I returned home and saw a note scribbled out: *Call Mel. Immediate. Important!* I knew that that meant he'd received his visa for Iran. I tried not to seem alarmed, though soon he would enter a country where human life meant nothing, where children were sent to walk across mine fields.

"Now I won't see you for another month," I complained, reminding him that I had to leave for Zurich right before his return.

"Don't take my sweater to Europe," he said.

"What?" I asked.

"Just don't take my sweater with you."

Suddenly I felt alone, with or without his sweater. I knew we were talking about the sweater instead of admitting how frightened we were.

"And if he gets killed you can keep it!" my son yells.

"I don't have to wear it again."

But now his voice was loving and calm, "I want it to be where it is."

I wore his sweater to bed that night, sort of like having the last word, but when I woke up, I knew I should wear my own clothes. I would go out and find my own sweater. It would be red with a design around the yoke. This new red sweater I had in mind would be my own chosen garment, the emblem of a woman living alone in the woods, dressed to live, dressed to go on, no matter what. This one wouldn't be glamorous. It would almost be rough. But that's the way it's got to be these days.

And yet tonight as I sit here warmed by the fire, my feet are growing cold, and I'm still wearing his sweater, for I've grown accustomed to it. No doubt it will find its way into his hands, though it might not fit him now, any more than my over-sized love. But maybe some night he'll feel the urge to go sleep with it — he'll go into his closet and dig it out, wrap it around him as I have done, to keep him together, and warm.

THE TRAP

I'm not calling to find out if he's at work. I'm calling to find out why he isn't. He's been working seven days a week for the past two months, trying to get this film cut.

I ask the hotel operator for his room, and half expect him to answer, "Hey," but a woman's voice has another impact.

"Is Ron there?" I ask.

She groans. I've woken her. "I guess he left," she says. Brilliant.

"Is this Mona?" I ask, knowing that will awaken her.

I once teased him by saying he'd been moaning for Mona all night in his sleep, pure invention, but he retorted, "You mean Mona from the hospital?" For a second I didn't know if she were real or not.

"This is Jennifer," she answers. Sounds like one. "Do you want to leave a message?"

"Just tell him that Mona called," I say to further confuse things. "Tell him he has no need to call back. I'll come get my stuff. He can leave my coyote in the closet."

"Oh," she says. "I thought that belonged to his girlfriend."

Not it's my turn for confusion.

I have the key to his room in my wallet. It looks like a thin cardboard credit card, with a picture of a key and perforated holes — this is your modern key — not a real object with character and weight, something that turns a real lock, no real true lasting love at the Sheraton. But I stick it down the slot one last time, watch the green light flash, then push down.

It had become more and more apparent that he didn't like the way I dressed. He made subtle comments at first, window shopping, "You'd look great in that," severe black outfits with radical skirts. One time I got the look just right, a blue-black oversized jacket with plenty of shoulders, tight black pants. He couldn't stop raving, "Just look at yourself. It's terrific! Now you look thirty, not like some kind of matron."

Suddenly I worried about age. Wrinkles became an obsession. I checked out everybody's face, the way lines had formed on older people compared to mine, those just beginning etch marks, little crescents around the mouth. I was not a frivolous person, so why not accept some worry lines. I was a real person who did her own laundry. Ron worried about losing hair. He had plenty of it, and I couldn't care less, but he was a hawk for wrinkles. Vanity made him want *me* to look good.

I feel disgust for the burnt sienna which overwhelms the hotel room—carpet, paper, drapes. The maid has been here already, tidy bed, clean ashtrays. In fact it doesn't even smell like smoke. Maybe he hasn't been sleeping here. He certainly didn't beg "Mona" for a second chance.

I call him at work after my little conversation with Jessica. For a second he's not sure who I am. I'm calling from Florida in a sun-drenched mood. "How's your weekend going?" I ask.

"All right," he answers, distracted. I've interrupted him, I feel.

"You wouldn't believe my tennis," I say. "And I'm swimming fifty laps. I've never felt so fit."

"Are you getting tan?"

"Yes, but it makes me horny. Why do you have to work so hard?"

"That's life," he says, resigned. "But listen, this is a hectic time right now. I'm trying to finish the sound track with Neal."

"How was she?" I ask. "I mean, your date."

"What is it with you," he sounds angry. He never answers questions like this one directly.

He'd said repeatedly how he hadn't slept with anyone since the day he met me. I tried to overlook the messages left on his machine, "Oh Ronny, I miss you *so much* . . . At the sound of *my* beep, leave a message on *my* machine . . . Take care of your beautiful self, Ronald . . ." or that simple, sweet, seductive, "Hi . . ." as if the world should know who that is.

"You have no reason to be jealous," he states, "and frankly I'm in no mood for it this morning."

"Mood!" I warn him. "MOOD! I just wanted to let you know I just spoke to Janicka." Silence on the other end. "You're so full of shit my head's running over!" Silence on my end, breathing, deep battled breathing.

"You've got it all wrong," he says. "I can tell you're upset, but you're wrong."

I am dying for a believable excuse.

"I didn't sleep with her, I just let her use my room. I spent the night in Neal's other bed. Talk to him. She's up here for a dental conference."

"Why did she say you just left?"

"I went up to *change* this morning, OK? She's just an old college friend, ask Neal. The three of us had dinner together." He waited. "Kate?" I was waiting too. "If you can't believe me, what good is this."

"Listen, she told me everything. She was sleepy and had her defenses down. I threw her off balance by asking for Mona."

"Who?"

"We even laughed about your handsome *schlong*."

"*What!*"

"Do I need to reiterate what you already know? She even told me her bra size."

Once I had asked him, "Do you like big tits?" And he had said, "*No,* I hate them." But his male friends knew he liked "dairy," and I was skimpy on top, but Jennifer with her jambalayas, her big billowy cushions, I could picture him checking her out in the lobby—That woman is well put together. How he'd approach that part of her softly at first, but undressed he would almost ravish them. He'd suck them and squish them and push them together, adore them and look at them jiggle, and make them swing, and watch them hang — milk them and pinch them and fuck them and take them — swallow them whole, Great Tits!

It's 10 a.m. Sunday morning, Eastern Standard Time for us both. I had bad dreams last night, a bout of insomnia, because he hasn't called in two days. I need to hear his voice. I break the rule I've made for myself and call him anyway. He answers, "Hey." He is usually up for work by now.

"You told me to call when I had something to say, and you know how rare that is."

He makes an animal sound. I've awoken him. "I really tied one on last night," he admits. "I thought I could sleep it off." He's holding up a finger to his lips, indicating to the girl beside him that she should keep quiet. "Can I call you back," he says, "after I shower?"

"Well, I'm going to be out all day. We rented a boat. The boys want to fish."

But the girl is impatient, and I hear her whine, a rustle in the background, my excellent ears. "What's that?" I ask.

"What's *what?*" he answers.

"Someone's with you," I say.

"Will you knock if off, Kate. Nobody's with me."

"Liar," she whispers.

"I'll call you back," he squeezes her arm, she says, "*Ow!*"

"No need to," I say. "Not ever."

"Fine!" he yells, dropping the receiver on the floor, and I'm left there listening, mutely listening, as he proceeds to grapple with her. I hear their struggle — He's tickling her and pinning her down — her groans, her sighs, her stretching calls, being stroked and bent and taken. Then I get to hear her slobbering over him, her drooling, muttering, praising, until his final, "*unnn.*"

I often felt thirsty in this hotel room. Maybe it was the

altitude, or lack of real air. It felt like sleeping on an airplane. I bought a humidifier, which seemed to help, but now the room feels dry.

I tear the bedding from the huge, neat bed, trompling on it merrily. I get my hair curler set from the bottom drawer. He didn't like to see my hair done. He had gotten to that "admitting phase." He preferred my hair all messed up, wild looking, as if I'd spent the day in bed. Like when?

I stuff my clothes in the duffle, no time to fold, but the coat, my coyote, isn't hanging in the closet. Did he have the nerve to still wear it? That coat made him look like a hunk with big shoulders, made him look like the filmmaker he was, with his torn t-shirt and three-day beard. I loved the way he looked.

Calmly, deliberately, I wreck the room, sweep the side tables clean of spare change, empty cigarette boxes, canister of pills, hotel information flying, then notice that my letters are gone. He had always left them out before, as proof of his fidelity, that no other girl could be brought to this room, with love notes prominently displayed.

I dump out the drawers, the neatly rolled t-shirts, socks, underwear. The hotel does his laundry. He never cooks food. Clean sheets and towels daily. I place the key card on the middle of the naked bed. The bare mattress looks peculiar, virginal, like an unused diaphragm, rubbery and functional. The pillows are far and wide.

Shutting the door to the hotel room, I feel a momentary pang, a panic, that maybe I can get back in, put everything back together, remake the bed, forgive him, and I'd be there napping when he returned, the humidifier breathing with moisture. I test the door. It's sealed. Now the humidifier's empty. I guess he doesn't fill it anymore.

I decide to call Neal from the lobby. I'll get him to make the exchange of coats outside their office building, blocks away. Neal will want to help prevent a scene.

"Don't say anything to Ron," I insist. "I just want what's mine then I'm out of here."

Neal says, "OK." I think he's secretly glad that it's come to his. Ron liked to call Neal, "My wife." Both of them found that amusing. They found endless fault with most women — waitresses, editors, over-wrought girlfriends. They had slept with too many to know what they wanted. Perhaps Ron needed some composite touch, taken from the very best qualities of all the women he'd ever been with. Well, I guess she's out there somewhere, with her teenage legs and high-fashion mind, but she's getting older too.

When I reach the revolving door, Neal isn't waiting. The guard is sitting at the desk as usual. Silent, grey tomb of a place. Chilly. Then Ron walks out of the elevator with an unlit smoke in his mouth, wearing my coat, fucking wearing it! I back away as he revolves outward. I am too furious to speak. He lights the thing and turns away from me, as if I wanted to admire his profile. "You can have it when I'm finished with this," he says, meaning the smoke.

"You *are* finished." I knock it out of his mouth.

He looks at me imitating my *very-mean-look,* and slowly starts to unbutton it, lets it slide from his shoulders onto the ground. I pretend to turn away and then *whack* him. He trips backwards over the coat, knocks his hand against the concrete slab of wall — then cradles his arm as if injured.

"Hey," he says, "it's me."

"Hi," I answer, yawning.

"It's Sunday you know, and I missed you this morning."

"I miss you too."

"How are you?" he asks. "Getting sun burned?"

"I couldn't sleep last night."

"You should have called me," he insists.

"I didn't think you'd appreciate a press conference, not at three a.m."

"That's true," he chuckled. "How're the boys."

"They're fine, but I don't like travelling alone."

"You're not alone. Are you still coming home tomorrow? I have to go back to the hospital."

"Will you call me? I want to know what the doctor says."

"Sure, I'll call."

"Well you didn't for two days," I accuse him.

"You know where I am."

I don't answer this.

"You sound upset," he says.

"I'm just not smoking."

"Good, don't smoke."

"I love you," I say.

"I love you too." He's not just miming me. "And I'm tired of working. Next trip we go together. I've got to get back in shape. Kate? Are you there?"

"Yes, I was just thinking."

"You think too much. Relax."

"I can't relax when you tell me to."

"You know I've been staying at this hotel for so long, we've got a cruise coming on our extended stay card or whatever this thing is."

"For two?" I ask.

"Just me and you," he rhymes, to put me in a better mood. "I'm going to take you around the world. How would you like that?"

ON THE LINE

At the wedding of my cousin, my aunt stood up and spoke about an omen. She believed in them. So did I. So I listened to her toast more closely.

She said that the groom had come to visit her and he'd left his trunks on the line. Big red trunks, but they had faded, clipped to the line for several seasons.

It wasn't until spring that she noticed that a bird had built a nest in them. And then the bird went on to make a family — inside the dangling apparatus of his swimming trunks. And so she toasted to the groom.

My boyfriend came to the wedding. He met my entire family and got up on water-skis for the first time. "Thank God," I thought, since my brothers were standing on the pier in their big watchful bodies. Thank God he was able to do it. Even if he did wear a different kind of swimming trunks — tight, as if to show off the equipment he was born with.

When we returned back east, he confessed to the husband of my best friend, that he thought I'd give an ultimatum soon. We'd been dating for over a year now. My boyfriend said, that if I put it to him, he would probably have to say, "Yes."

Later I told him I would give no ultimatum. I didn't want a man who needed one. The vase, for me, was broken.

I said all this because of disappointment, that he hadn't made a step in my direction. I felt that he had had his chance. I was trying to get some response, forced into a mean state of mind — trying to maintain control, and of course that left me more helpless than I cared to be.

Because something basic was always missing with us, jealousy filled in the spaces. I spied marks on the sheets. I announced he felt chaffed, and knew why he was exhausted. I didn't mind being ridiculous. Sooner or later it would all be confirmed. I'd arrive and it didn't seem to matter. I wasn't felt to be a missing part.

So now I dream of packages exploding. Perhaps giving too much has done this to me. I would rather crawl back to my mailbox. I no longer retain the panic seizure to flee. It is more like staying very quiet, knowing that the life has gone out of this, like wind dropping out of those pants on the line when the air becomes strange and still. And I remember I did find a dead bird once under our bed and wondered if it were a sign.

THE MALLORY

When Samuel was a child, he lived with his father and mother in The Mallory, Central Park West.

But Samuel was no longer a child. Or was he. Samuel was forty-four, and for some reason never got married or bought a house or owned a car or raised a pet or had a child, not to mention a long-term relationship. I was his girlfriend and found out why.

"In those days, women always dressed up," Samuel described his mother. "I can still remember her easing on these long, leather gloves. She'd wear half-veiled hats and perfect, tailored suits."

"You watched your own mother getting dressed?" I imagined him sitting on their double bed, high above the parquet floor, while she wandered around in her slip, making-up.

My own mother leapt for a towel, when I came into her bathroom.

But Samuel and his mother were in cahoots. Only they knew the script — with her monkey face grimace behind the back of his father, Samuel rolling around with laughter.

Samuel's mother made a habit of lunching with her girlfriends, and often she took Samuel along, her diminutive escort. These women were so well put together that they'd sneer at anyone who wasn't — "I wonder where in the world she got *that.*"

"He was the light of her life," Samuel's father explained, and I could see that light still shining in Samuel's eyes as he silently communed with his mother, as she lay in intensive care.

She refused to even look at me.

"He was the most important person in her life from the day he was born," Bernard said.

"I'm sure you were just as important, Mr. Rosenthal," I put in, but he was no dummy and knew what was what.

"Nothing compared to Samuel. He was such a happy child."

This was not a happy adult. At times I could see a remnant of the boy still trapped beneath his balding scalp, bouncing around on well-kept calves, but such apparitions weren't pleasant.

Samuel used to work for *She She,* a women's magazine. He was the art director, one of the few straight men in that beehive of beauties, and oh the stories he could tell — how they would *use men* to collect expensive dinners, swoop on merchandise and finagle free trips, spread their skinny legs for even the least promotion, but did any one of them have true style?

He described his mother as if she were a breathing beauty. As if every line of her moved uptown in perfect city elegance and feminine authority — black, severe, and chic.

It was only later, when his mother's life hung in question that I spoke to the disinherited sister. "I'm sure Sam'll take care of everything," she said. "I'll be happy when the old bitch dies."

He was furious that I'd answered the phone and gotten into a conversation. But I thought it wrong that he hadn't gone to his only nephew's bar mitzvah, that he refused to speak to his sister as if guarding the inheritance, one of the ten best views of the city.

The Mallory had two elevators, one for residents and one for domestics. The Rosenthals had a laundress. Her name was Lily and she came every week. She washed, she dried, she ironed and folded. But one week Lily had a funeral to attend, so Mrs. Rosenthal decided to do the laundry herself.

Wheeling out her heap of clothes, she looked more like the cleaning lady than the proprietress. She pushed the rolling basket into the elevator that would take her down to the basement.

This is how Samuel told it. He could drag a story out and make everybody impatient, saying, "You know what I mean," too many times. Of course, in his version, his mother remained well-dressed, perfumed, a sophisticate.

She rode in the elevator as always, just as she was used to doing. "Lily sick this morning?" asked the elevator man, before dropping her in the unfamiliar dimness of the basement.

How Samuel and I hooked up is beyond me now, for here I am living deep in the country, citronella my favorite cologne, training Morgans and boarding other people's horses. Nothing gives me greater pleasure than to see a couple of dark bay colts kicking up across the pasture.

OK, perhaps I can muck out the stalls in the morning, and later cook a five course meal, wear a little black dress if I have to, but I'd rather stay put in my blue jeans and go to bed early. I'd rather, as I told him late in the relationship, "I'd rather ride alone."

I think Samuel dropped into my life instead of a midlife crisis. But there weren't enough people on Seekonk Road to appreciate the way he looked. He needed an audience and a pat on the head. I already had enough girlfriends.

Samuel had dated a majority of the girls at *She She,* one pretty editor after another, but they were either too this or too that. With me he had the excuse of distance, conflicting styles, "The country is so *creepy.*"

Then a new editor-in-chief was called in, Dan Heller, and he wanted to reorganize the magazine staff.

Dan and Donna Heller also lived at The Mallory, but they only lived on the 14th floor.

"Do you know how long my parents have lived in that apartment? Do you know how low their mortgage is? Even I could afford it."

"Is that where you want to live?" I asked him, wondering what would draw a man back to his baby bed.

I wanted him, at that point, to move in with me. He

could continue with his freelance photography. That's how we met. He was doing a piece on weekend people, *"Barbecue of the Vanities,"* and he thought my horses looked bucolic. He liked the way I sat on a fence.

The Hellers were relatively new to The Mallory, but Donna Heller seemed to know the rules. On the day Mrs. Rosenthal ascended from the basement with her basket of laundry, Mrs. Heller was waiting at ground level in her rather trendy suit, ready to rise to her much lesser view of the same green park in three directions.

When Mrs. Heller saw this bent old lady with grey frizzy hair in the residents' elevator with a heaping load of laundry, she tried to remain polite. "I'm afraid," she glanced at the elevator man, "we have another machine in the building for laundry."

Mrs. Rosenthal didn't say anything.

"You shouldn't be on this elevator," Donna Heller persisted, until Mrs. Rosenthal was forced to look up at her.

"What, only bitches can ride?" she said, before her clean load of laundry ascended to the very top floor of The Mallory.

In the hospital I asked her if she and Samuel were ever in collusion, and she said, "Yes."

"Against whom?" I asked.

"Against Bernard."

Samuel now worked for *Faire,* a women's magazine. They liked his expertise. But now if I wanted to see him, I drove to the city and ate dinner around midnight. Of course I still woke at 6 a.m.

I discovered that Samuel had to call his father every morning. "Why call if it makes you upset?" I asked.

"To see if he's still alive."

"Samuel, your father's a macrobiotic. He's going to outlive the whole lot of us."

"He thinks it's a son's obligation. That I should take care of my mother, not him."

"That's warped," I said. "Just tell him to shove it. Tell him you'll call when you really *feel* like talking." I realized he'd be kissing goodbye his inheritance, and I wanted to say — So what.

"He's ruining my fucking life!" Samuel marched down the hall in his maroon bathrobe, followed by an exhale of smoke. "Did you know he even tried to kill her? I found bed sores this deep! I had to call off the cops. I should have let them cart off the old shithead."

Bernard Rosenthal seemed fairly harmless to me, but he did have an opinion on everything.

"Plus! He's ruining that fucking apartment!"

Mr. Rosenthal had glaucoma. He liked to stay in and listen to Mozart. He rarely ventured out. He no longer employed a housekeeper, not to mention a laundress. He believed the cleaning process ruined good clothes. He didn't like his personal life disturbed, his privacy invaded.

"Garbage, dirt, dishes, laundry, newspapers, records, grime, filth! And he can't even fucking see it!" Samuel yelled, screaming at that landfill in the sky.

Samuel himself was immaculate. He had gotten impatient with me as well. "Don't open that can on the counter. I'll do it. And don't answer the phone when I'm gone."

I believed there was another woman, but what could I do?

"Samuel was the love of her life," Mr. Rosenthal told me when I called up to say hi. "Ever since the day he was born. Such a happy child, and my wife just adored him. My wife, she lived in the moment. No one ever enjoyed living so much. Samuel had a great education, this city. People were meant to live together in the city."

"I'd never raise a child in this environment," I told him. "Children need freedom and animals."

Freedom he had, but an animal? No. His father told him

that if he wanted a dog, he had to practice walking one on an empty leash, twice a day for three months.

"They went to the opera, museums, ballet," he was referring to Samuel and his mother, but then I remembered a disturbing event from my own childhood.

My father took me to the Chicago Symphony. It was our one big date, and I was all dressed up in black velvet, hair curled. We sat in the orchestra and I was thrilled. But before the music was finished, by intermission I was sobbing, "Where are the tunes!" As if he had betrayed me.

"I don't want you talking to that fuckhead!" Samuel yelled.

"He was just telling me about his childhood."

Samuel didn't like this, because Bernie Rosenthal was a self-made man. He had pulled himself up by the bootstraps, all the way up to the top floor of The Mallory, where Samuel liked to imagine his history began, not on the lower east side with the immigrants.

"He said when he was young he played this game with himself. He'd throw up his cap and wherever it landed, he'd go in that direction. When he felt like taking another turn, he'd throw up his cap again."

"He never told me anything like that," Samuel said.

Just then the phone began to ring, and his body tensed. He let it ring, and it rang and rang. We were both sitting there on the bed just watching it, and finally I picked it up and said, "Hi," but nobody answered, nobody spoke. I handed him the receiver and said loudly, "Don't you even want to say hello?"

THE ONE THING YOU CAN'T HAVE

When I come back to the lake I refuse to stay in the big house. So does my brother, Bobbie, and Daba, his wife. Dorie is forced to move out of the garage apartment with her three small sons, into my mother's summer house with its twelve spacious bedrooms and lake view. Nobody wants to stay there.

Bobbie's standing by the big screen window, checking the drive. "Here she comes," he comments, seeing our mother ride by in her golf cart, "the happiest woman on earth." The golf cart's electric and makes no sound. Sometimes that can be startling.

Dorie seems frantic, running around. She wants to make things right for a change. I wish she'd give up, but it's our sister's theory that our father never loved our mother properly, that he's responsible for her behavior.

It's true, our father in his dotage, prefers the company of glamorous young people. He likes to take them riding, to make a big fuss, and mother's always been jealous of his least attention.

"It's hard to include someone," I say, "who'd rather sit for hours on her martini boat reading religious pamphlets."

"I swear to God," my brother says, "I'll have a party on that boat when she kicks the bucket."

"Don't hold your breath," I say.

I skirt her house while heading for the lake front.

"I don't know why your father has to work," she calls, "the one week you're home to visit."

I hear a door slam, children shrieking. Dorie's having a hard time keeping her sons in line, and as far as their grandmother's concerned — "Children are overrated."

Bobbie and Daba have a boy and a girl. Helen's my favorite. Her long colt legs gallop her around, and she has a gift for music.

"Can you drink a horse's milk?" she wants to know, before slipping through the side door of the big house to play the grand piano. I know the smell of that room—my mother couldn't change that. It smells cooler than the rest of the house, vaguely like pewter and leather-bound books. Helen plays a Beethoven Sonatina, I can hear it from the path—like sunlight falling through small wet leaves. But suddenly the music stops.

When she catches up to me, she says, "Gramma was napping."

"My grandmother," I tell her, "your Great-Gramma Helen, used to have the most beautiful garden on the lake. The gardener, old Kirchner, used to say that she ordered every single item in the seed catalogue." There used to be a buoyancy to the black glacial earth carefully worked in the garden, but now grass grows over as if it were a tomb.

"So what do you think of the decorating I did in the apartment?" my mother asks from her porch.

"Actually, I don't mind the pink floors so much, but the wallpaper's got to go."

"The room needed something," she acts insulted, as if I never appreciate anything, justifying her violation, for she entered what was considered "my place" and though Dorie and her family now live there in the summer, I was the one who fixed it up, back when Gramma was alive.

"My great-grandparents," I tell Helen, "your great-great-grandparents, were the only couple on the lake to have 'his' and 'her' chauffeurs. The drivers lived up here in this apartment, but that was years ago."

I was the oldest granddaughter and my grandmother's

favorite. She wanted to give me this garage apartment, but my father said no for tax reasons.

But I was the one who went in single-handed, sanded the floors and varnished them. Now they are pink. I tiled the kitchen and bathroom, painted every room and paid for that skylight.

When I moved back east, I came to the lake less often, and it was natural to pass the place along to Dorie, but my mother came in and removed my effects as if I had no business being there. I found my precious horse collection and demitasse set junked together with old pots and pans. It was as if I'd never placed that round, red armchair in the corner of my all-white bedroom, with those restful walls and plastered ceilings. I often sat in that chair and listened to the rain. My grandmother gave me that armchair. It was velvet and the back curved into the arms as if it wanted to embrace me.

When I returned this summer, I was surprised to see the chair sitting downstairs in the garage with a slipcover straining over it. It smelled musty, like a mattress gone bad, so much humidity here in the summer.

"Somebody's stolen my ring!" My mother starts the alarm. "My opal as well as my best scarab bracelet!"

All the *au pair* girls are in question, especially that one from Denmark, who'd just been let go. She had told the *au pair* girl from England, "By the end of this summer, I'll have that man in bed," meaning poor Dorie's husband.

Later when my mother finds her jewelry, she doesn't apologize.

My sister is on the verge of needing a sleep cure. "I just can't do this," she says to me. "Next time I'll pitch a tent."

When my mother drives off, I get Bobbie to help me and we go through the big house, rearranging everything, changing paintings and switching their chests-of-drawers around. We are pleased as punch with ourselves.

Yet I notice, as I go, I experience this greed, as if I wanted

69

to steal some object, something that was never given to me.

Our father tells us that we should jot down which items in the house appeal to us, so that he can put them in his will. Then he mentions, *hush-hush*, that Nico, his assistant, requested ·a Tiffany vase. Our father went ahead and mailed it, since Nico now lives in New York, and our father wonders if mother will find out, if she'll ever notice it missing.

"He gave *what* to *whom*?" says Dorie.

But I say, so what. Our father's always been extravagant, overly generous with us.

I announce that I only want the painting of Gramma, young Helen before the lake front, with her long dark hair pulled back with a ribbon, her full white dress and direct blue stare.

He says, "Unfortunately, that's the one thing you can't have." He's bequeathed it to the art museum. I had no idea it was worth that much, but my mother laughs as if I'd wanted to auction it.

"He never said no to her, you know what I mean?" Dorie explains. "He never gave her any limits. He just throws her these decorating bones. Anything to keep her quiet."

Our mother came into our grandmother's house and changed every room for the worse. She now locks all doors when she leaves the big house. This can be troublesome for Dorie.

This afternoon Dorie appears with a sleeping toddler in her arms. "Locked out," she apologizes. "Do you mind?"

"I can not believe this," I confront my father. "Why don't you send her on a trip!"

"You pay too much attention," is his reply. "You always have. Just ignore her."

In fact he did suggest a Scandinavian cruise, but she's no fool and knows what's what. "I'm not being run off my own place. I'm not going to have them come here and ruin my property."

But we are the ones who love the country, who swim every day and call it amniotic. We walk the overgrown paths to the remains of hiding places. We are the ones who come back to smell the algae and water-logged planks of the boathouse, feel the same old bounce of the tennis chairs, the nights so dark, flashing with electrical heat. We are the ones who attempt to retrieve a remnant of a reasonable childhood and end up bitching about her.

Helen whispers in my ear, "I know where she hides the keys to the golf cart." We sneak in and get them. I let Helen drive. Silently we roll across the lawn, endless lawn, until Helen smacks into a hickory and Matthew falls out, causing a bit of an uproar.

When my father takes Dorie riding, she asks to hold her baby son for a moment—but then Dad shoots the bug spray and Brilliance starts rearing and the baby flies, while Dorie lands sideways, gashing the back of her head.

Dorie feels it's his way of rejecting her. "He never protected us, you know. And he'd rather ride with someone else anyway."

His companions do have a tendency to fall, and I'm afraid one may eventually sue him.

"What a stupid way to lose your inheritance," Bobbie adds, though our father has always been generous. I want him to be able to simply live his life.

One time he took me to the stable. I had agreed to ride his new gelding, and there was a golden chain around the horse's neck. God, I thought, he's getting queer for this animal. But it was a necklace from Verona for me.

"Dad wants us to meet him in town for dinner," Dorie says. But we'd like to go shopping first. We're stuck here with only Dorie's station wagon, and Mom's two-seater Alfa. We don't want to drag the kids along. I try to explain this to our mother.

"Dorie and I would like to go in early. Do you think you could bring the kids later, in the station wagon?"

"Nobody borrows my car."

Oh, I forgot, bitches ride alone.

I decide to make a huge spaghetti dinner instead, and invite the whole family, including cousins next door, my aunt and uncle, all the babies and dogs. It's terribly hot to be boiling water, but I let the sauce simmer and make garlic bread too. Dorie buys red wine and Daba makes a salad. Bobbie offers to steal raspberry sherbet from the big house. We all work together and the children are happy, swinging on the swinging bed.

Then Helen plays a duet with her father. Bobbie was paid to take lessons as a child. It is clear that she adores him, as daughters are wont to do, though her talent for music far exceeds his.

I inherited my father's passion for horses, his need to escape. "Some people are best alone," I once said.

But then Mom butted in, "She's got terrible taste in men anyway."

My father, like me, likes a big family dinner, lots of commotion, more the merrier, we say. I invited our mother, knowing she'd never come — too noisy for dinner, too hot upstairs.

While we all sit around the big wooden table, spinning our noodles and helping ourselves to more cheese, more wine, more everything, we can't help but notice her as she rides by in her golf cart, a stenciled expression on her face. Is she going for the evening paper, or listening to the sound of our laughter? Who cares.

"Remember when we planted marijuana in the tomato patch?" I say to my cousin. "And then one of the old ladies from The Garden Club spotted it and told the police?" We hoot over that.

"But they couldn't arrest old Kirchner." He was God's baby. He'd come out of the greenhouse and ask you point blank—Have you seen My Lord? As if you might have just missed him. God smiles on everything, old Kirchner said, and sometimes I thought I knew what he meant, when I was riding bareback in my bathing suit with the sun all over me. But sometimes I thought he was weird.

Our father makes a toast to togetherness. We're all getting drunk and the sauce is delicious.

"Where's Gramma tonight?" Matthew asks.

"She doesn't eat pasta," I said, "not since she choked on that *pasta putanesca.*"

"She got the Heimlich maneuver right there in the restaurant," my brother puts in.

"I was there," Dorie said. "She gave the man twenty dollars."

"I've got one," Bobbie laughs. He's loose enough. "Do you know the difference between a slut and a bitch?"

"Bobbie!" Daba says. But no we don't, and yes, we'd like to.

"Well a slut is someone who'll sleep with anyone. And a bitch, is someone, who'll sleep with everyone, but You!"

Matthew wants to swim, and Grampa promises the children we'll all take a skinny dip later, but first we've got to have dessert. I remember how we used to scream with laughter in the dark, running and slipping on the white planks of the pier.

Then Dorie points down to the driveway, and my brother stands up. Our mother is sitting in her stationary golf cart with this message to deliver—"We haven't made love in twelve years! How do you like that?" She then jolts away, and our father pretends that he hasn't heard, clapping his hands once together.

"Let's have some music," he suggests, and Helen is eager. She skips into the end room and faces the upright. How she can see the notes is beyond me, but no one moves to turn a light on. We are deep in our sherbet, so sweet and so cold, as she easily begins *Für Elise.* It reminds me of something.

Possibly Bobbie played it as a child, but it takes me back and makes me think of my Gramma, the memory of the music moving through this small child, bringing faces and emotion to the surface of the water. We are silent, in awe, it should bring us great happiness, but instead it moves me further away, further and further away.

P A R T   T W O

THE NEVER ENOUGH CLUB

I *wake up thinking* — On Fire — *in every house, each hour. I write with my pen* — Tiger Tiger, *mount my horse and go, to the deepest river, lake's bend, submerge this rider in coolest water, hear the sizzle, and feel it soothe my fiery horse and I. Mouth in cinder, lips burn* — *Further and further we swim, pawing and floating* — *bobbing and stroking, until he rises with a shaking mane* — *I'm holding on and steaming with this animal between my legs.*

"I'm in love with my therapist," I tell my girlfriend.

"That's good," she says. "Everybody is." She knows what there is to tell. "So what are you going to do? Wait until therapy's over? That could take years." She knows me too well.

"What *can* I do," I shrug. Here I am club president, an extremist living in abstinence. If my friend wants to join she has to do something raw.

"Like what," she wants to know.

"Like shower in the men's room, I don't know, enter a pig catching contest, saunter into the blackest part of town, betray your primary school education. Use your head — maul a man."

Enough is getting to be too much.

"Start your own club then," I say, but she gets equally snotty.

"You think falling in love so much is some kind of record? You think you're gonna win a prize?"

"Shut up," I say, "this is serious. Can you imagine my love within limits?"

"So what does *he* have to say about this."

"Well you know when I first told him, I could hardly *breathe,* and he was so kind, you know what he said? He said, 'Remember when we met by accident in front of that filling station? I was completely overwhelmed by how much I felt for you.' "

"No kidding."

But someone was approaching — his dun-colored wife. She saw that he looked flustered, and she appeared — grim.

So I started to dream and I brought them like offerings. *We are standing up front, witnessing a marriage but the wedding's postponed and then we're dancing in the treetops leaping and dancing while this owl watches on. When we come back down I say spur of the moment how much I love him but now he can't move — stuck in blue ski boots and he admits he's never loved anyone.*

"Jewel in the icebox," she says.

But he was made for music. I can hear it like a halo, hovering around him. I have seen him in my basement touching my piano. He wanders through my house which is spicey full of light a little messy you know like a flower arrangement that has opened and loosened — a petal falling here — a petal there — soft dusting of pollen.

"But maybe he's just curious about you," she says. "Don't you find it offensive, being referred to as a time-slot? You *are* his two o'clock, right?"

"I just want him to love my basement!" I scream.

"Everybody else does, why wouldn't he?"

"Because he's different, like a sandwich."

"What do you mean, like a sandwich?"

Well we are sitting on the sofa (feet up) yin-yang facing each other and I've been adoring the baby with his same-name before the fag-hag babysitter comes with too much make-up. I'm afraid he says as if I might corrupt him though (I) once was the sacrificial lamb.

"Maybe he's afraid of losing his dun-colored wife. She's kept him together so far, sacrificed *her* desire for babies, and

78

he's probably developed a conscience along the way. I bet *he'd* confess to having eaten that chocolate covered egg wrapped in goldleaf left in the front hall bowl."

And then a bunch of wild horses appears and the leader picks up my horse by the scruff of his neck and carries him around the way a mother might — it looks painful to me and I peel out riding bareback extremely fast no saddle or bridle I steer with the mane down a treacherous with potholes and puddles dirt road but I make it escape and then this stallion's a guy and his name is Guy also and we're happy reunited not made of ceramic.

"Sounds like an engagement," she congratulates me.

But what am I going to do, I wonder, with all these golden apples?

"More than one way to win a woman," she adds, in her tiny, Chinese voice.

So here we are in another realm, like those sugared eggs with inside scenes, and yes, the scent of hot sweetness is in the room — it's cooking between us, though the wedding's been postponed and I'm losing patience addressing invitations to everybody in the whole wide world.

"Maybe this is a kind of dress-rehearsal," she offers. "You're always taking off your clothes."

She wants to see *me* courted for a change. She wants to see *him* ride up on *his* steed bringing flowers for *me* for instance.

I look out the window as if he might appear, but then the telephone rings and it's *her* boyfriend. Everybody else seems to live on the outside. Even his dun-colored wife. She reaches for his napkin, that intimate. Peas on the pony, my food.

I ask him if he still sleeps with her and he admits that they share the same bed but that he sleeps on the edge and doesn't touch her anymore. That reassures me — though he is so close to falling I have to almost hold my breath.

"They might no longer have sex," she reminds me, "but they do share an icebox and an answering machine. That's what bigger boys are made of."

79

"But with me," I retort, "he'd sleep in the middle. He'd discover what it's like to swim a horse double, feel the animal bounding, the rise and the fall of it, plunging and laughing — coming up with a shout."

I told him I talk to my animals. I call my dog, Pussygirl. I told him my horse takes comfort in my arms, leans the weight of his head upon my shoulder. I'm blind in one eye. Would he find that unusual?

"Just tell me," she asks, "do they stir-fry food?"

"I betcha they use those new-age briquets made of mesquite I betcha."

Sometimes I think my inside world has moved outside, and all of the outside has entered in. It's like my love is riding Out There, in nature, and the natural world's a watercolor on my one good retina, mimetic of my feelings for him.

Sometimes I identify with whole families eating from a bucket of Kentucky Fried Chicken, normal folks taking a fast walk together in a line along the road, on a kind of march, or in the ice cream parlor with the small town girls checking out a stranger. Beauty is threatening. I want to reveal! Submerge in sensation. I anoint myself with Oil of Memory, slippery in the heat of summer therapy, pumping inside. I felt the jolt, I swear. Out there on the sidewalk before the filling station.

"Did he say — Fill 'er up?"

"Very funny," I answer. "This is a different kind of longing, manifesto part two, for completion on a much more *spiritual* level."

"Oh slime on the pond."

But he can help me move through this. Give a shove, canoe stuck in weeds.

Before I know it I'm shooting like a torpedo through the ocean at an upwards angle with this monster fish mouth opening at my heels and I know I've been stung I can feel the poison but I keep my legs straight together like this so when the fish takes a bite I explode through her hymen and I am conceived.

"This makes me uneasy."

"Pre-seismic! Exactly—what we're afraid to look at—Daddy's scrotum exposed when the towel folds open—it belongs to my therapist!"

"How can his wife put up with this. And you're paying," she insists. "You're paying for improvement."

"There's a cash flow," I admit, "but it keeps us clean."

"Clean-schmean. This is a business. He could list it in the phone book: Hire-A-Husband, and you'd pay and pay."

"He makes me feel loved."

"For an hour?" she bleats. "An hour's enough for you!"

"You don't understand. That hour lasts forever. I can see the sunrise set now, touch the swirls of the galactic, metamorphic milk, a new shine of radiance, much better than marriage."

"Sex has always been a commodity," she states bluntly, "but now it is love?"

"And I've got a prescription, the proper dose."

"Wait a minute, am I talking to the president?"

"This husband won't hit you," I defend my stance.

"Yeah," she concurs, "he won't even *touch* you."

But I know if I can love myself wholly, then I can love anybody. *So let me just lie here in the river for a while with my therapist beside me—it's very elemental—so clear and so liquid—no clothes are upon us as the water glides over us.*

"Even you," my friend tells me, "might have to grow up."

"I'm sure there are advantages to marriage," I answer, "but no one has pointed them out to me."

"You're looking at one." She figures she's the fruit of her parents' peaches, that won't stain. We're all two people in the same pants anyway.

"I think marriage came along like self-defense to shield something that's missing. So if my therapist will read the vows, I'll get married to myself and be divinely happy."

"With a real horse?"

"I already have a horse."

"And he has a wife, who doesn't *need* to hire a husband, she already has one."

"But they don't fuck."

"So what's it to you? King, Queen or Jack."

"It's not that I want to *rent* a man, but sometimes I *need* one and can't *find* one anywhere. If only somebody would *loan* me a man or possibly *give* me one for a short while. I wouldn't mind *borrowing* a husband, returning him later, and — Hey, I could use a little help getting this cork out of the champagne bottle, I never liked that pop in the face and a woman can't do everything plus would you mind helping with these new-age briquets for the grilled salmon anchovy butter brings out the flavor and it's so much easier to make a bed from both sides. *You* wouldn't want to start seeing my therapist, would you?"

"Not if he's saddled with a dun-colored wife and goes home to eat pot roast. People get stuck in their lives," she yells. "They can only go SO FAR. Can't you see that? Not everybody wants to join your club!"

"You mean, if he were to actually walk outside therapy, and step into my Isuzu Trooper II and drive with me over to that abandoned Colonial in the middle of the field did you know it's for sale a dream house I tell you we could live there someday raise horses write music compose big bouquets not to mention make other things, then something's going to fall apart?"

"Yeah, the illusion."

Well you know what? I've taken the jewels out of the icebox. They're melting. I'm defrosting the whitefish. I've put lights on my heels and I'm looking for a haircut for the New Me. I'm passing through the outside with love tipped on my ice skates, through the eye of the egg with violent storm warnings, kissing ears anyway. Fear has flooded the passageways for long enough. Food's weighed us down and now we're flying backwards into the past in a rolling convertible back to the married lives of both of our ancestors where life was simple as wooden tools *clonking* whole apples — half an eon ago — and we retrace those footsteps till silence is upon us — then we rise from the water like bride and groom.

But then out of the darkness comes a very old fellow pushing a wheelbarrow and I am thrilled. Is it true? I rush up to him. Is it true what they say? That everything that's brought out of this dark turns to gold?

KILLER GORILLA

I see a Killer Gorilla in my fine apartment — almost landing —
Have to HIDE small son in bathtub basement turn out the
lights and RUN!

Killer Gorilla is out on the terrace, probably in Paris, and
I'm my father's daughter, sender of postcards, trying to Sniff
fresh flowers in mist and beCOME a charmed individual.

My Big boy — Oh NO — gives the hiding place away — (little knees stick up like broccoli in the cooler bin). I warn him
WATCH OUT we've got a killer on the MOVE here and he's coming to GET US — (Don't shout!)

Am I sacrificing the hungry big teenager, to protect the
little broccoli boy? Gorilla says HE'LL choose his own body,
thank you. Thanks to yourself you stupid FUCK. Now we'll
probably ALL be dismembered.

Maybe I can put gorilla's head mask on and prepare to
babysit the baby. I AM Killer Gorilla in toy outfit, out to
devestate my rival — Gobble-gobble GIT OUT A HERE go back
to yer husband or over the balcony baby.

I'll smash the blue plastic conTAINer god Dammit, scare
the living Daylights out of everyone! Hey, seven counts of
assault for Seven Fake Sisters pulling on dyed, pretend gloves.
Rip 'EM OFF! Seven bitches for seven festering boils.

Here comes gorilla gettin' goin' now — no chaining HIM
down cause HE's in *LOVE*. No more a monster than what you
have made him, CRAZY and TERRIBLE — a Killer Gorilla
climbing all the way UP only to be shot down.

Perhaps if you kiss him, take the monster in your arms,
you won't have a killer on your hands, just wind-dried sheets,
sun-dried tomatoes, and a broken baby thermometer in your
mouth.

You'll have a *Farewell to Moms* above baroque dining area, a celebrity ski trip with the animus man. Movies, my meat. You won't go out anymore with no rain-stopping USER. Snap your purse shut on THAT, for you're rich, you're a killer. Knock 'em dead!

Serious and bookish you can drop out of school, bare your back and be kissed beside laundry and STILL be alone. Well all right. If somebody points out your weak spot—inherited wealth, give 'em a 14 carat chain with a charm of Empire State Building, Jessica Lange blow-up for a Blind Date, *schlag mit schlag,* a string of department stores where the salesgirls flutter at the sight of your name. HEY, somebody left a humble parcel of rosy red apples on my unmade bed.

Gorilla climbs out of her costume, hangs it on a hook, takes a crunch. It's DELICIOUS. Much better than those golden, inedible ones.

The boys pop out of the freezer chest, ready to take advantage of MY GOOD NATURE. But we won't abuse mother now WILL WE.

What's for supper, they say.

This pie, without crust.

These are the happiest days of my life, I confess, and the younger one says, he is already smiling—"Well I guess you're gonna just have to LIVE with it!"

LET THE LADY APE SPEAK

Let her speak, Come On — LISTEN. She's standing in her corner, beating on her breast, her blackened ape chest, *moaning*. She isn't articulate, but speaking from the deepest, dark nation of her CUNT. The thumping *clomp* of her fist might appear as: ME ME ME ME ME *ME*, but on closer inspection: YOU-*YOU*, YOU-*YOU*.

She might be a mutant but what are you, an IDIOT? Can't you tell this grrrilla girl's in pain? *Love* pain. And sometimes she feels it's Impossible, for No One will EVER love Her in return.

She's rippin' round the corner now to trash the place — Down on all four knees panting in childbirth, for OH-nly to be reborn not a monster — She cries to you ROARing to Hold her. She's going under she says — I'M GOING UNDER, then vomits up loads of black tar-like meconium.

Ah, but you were helping like a mother might have done if she'd ever had a mother Fuck YOU. She knows she's ridiculous imagining a lover and trying to make her ape face CUTE.

Would you scream if she turned her gorilla mug your way? Say UGH because she stinks of rank garlic? She's got the slippery puking smell of boiled chitlins under armpits and the stench of rotten scallops under skirt.

She knows she is Big, black and UGLY, not pretty in pink or well-parked. SHE knows. You dream about some bowling ball hair-do, for she hasn't got the proper war-drobe.

She takes off — with that slouch with that bulge in her brow, dirty ole diapers dragging. If only she could SPEAK it would be all French poetry — "A dappled mare became a mottled moth." Or, "Hummingbirds basting their two hems together," but the more she thinks the GRUNT much harder it is to TALK — That's Why She Goes On This Rampage!

Her blood is all black and her tongue has turned blue. Lesser than the least of your breed, Mr. Upright.

Have mercy on her brain for her dumpster's on empty. You fill it like a close-up on FRUIT. Cut her open — pull it out — Such TRASH in her refrigerator. She's been lifting all Sorts of junk.

She's a thief she's a liar. Just look at her SLOBBER. Innards are what she likes most. She dribbles on the toilet, snorts in her sleep, and is ready to just fuck your brains out.

She wants to cuddle on your shoulder, smell the male scent of Pear, hear a white man's (real slowed down) heart beat. But *HA* she's got the sheet up over her head now, so you can not see her humming like the dickens, and she wants to hear The Words — Whadya know?

You lie down beside her and say quiet, very quiet, almost inaudible, "I love you."

She stops chewing. Say WHAT? She didn't get it the first time. You repeat that you love her. OH NO. She grabs the keys from the ignition. She's got to GET OUT A HERE she knows she could only get HURT.

Tapping her heart with one hairy finger, she beats time with her purple brow. If you listen, you can hear the mountain bell in her breast, see the white Himalayas, and the little toy train, chugging up the impossible slope. She sits on the engine eating big chunks of coal, crying for her generation. For everyone is selfish. Selfish and afraid. And gorillas were *meant* to be lonely.

THE WOMAN I'D LIKE TO ELIMINATE

I don't wanna talk about it," I say to Jelena. "I'm not one of those love-too-much women. Not anymore."

We're raking up the chicken yard, and this one bird's got his head cocked around as if he'd just heard something. My boys are too busy to help me. They even sleep fast. While Jelena here is aiming to marry my ex-husband and needs some information. Me too.

Jelena's no flirt so it's hard for her to understand that Tyler and I were always soft on somebody. "But I never *did* anything, see?" I explain. "I just used it as a kind of inspiration." Love always put me in the mood for my music. "But with him now, he had to go through with it, and I had one hell of a nose."

Jelena is right furious with Ty. Her black wavy hair seems to kink up in coils, as if her thoughts were electrifying her. It certainly makes her work good, and I do like company when I got a job.

"So how's all the plans for the wedding?" I ask. I figure she's got something brewing.

"There ain't gonna be no wedding. Tyler's in love."

"Oh no," I say. Poor Jelena. She must know it's his only defense. It couldn't mean a thing, not really.

"It's the girl who types his things up in Lexington."

I immediately picture someone pretty like my sister, with all that luxurious gold hair. "What does she look like?" I ask.

"She looks exactly like you," Jelena says. "About fifteen years ago."

She means, not unkindly, when I was twenty pounds lighter, tall thin straight long dark brown hair. Secretly, I'm a little pleased. But how can Jelena not hate me?

"He sits around with his head in his hands, as if I'm

s'posed to feel sorry. I just wanna *kill him!*"

I believe she is serious. But I don't want her doing that in front of my children.

Daniel's been telling me not to eat so much so fast, but the younger one's on my side—"She's just good with a fork!" I got my reasons to put food away.

But lately I've been wondering about this woman name a Judith, and today is the day I mean to find out. Judith is this K-Mart clothes designer, who always had a crush on Ty. He thought if he was real outright I wouldn't suspect, but you don't go sharing a cigarette with somebody, placing it back in her mouth.

Well he always pretended there was nothing there, that Judith simply gave him clothes, seconds on sweaters she had some peons knit up for her, big faggoty pants, way too stylish for him. He looked best in a pair of worn levis, a soft flannel shirt. I didn't like him looking too prissy. But he was her highschool sweetheart, said "friend," and supposedly they had never slept together so they hadn't got it out of their system.

So then I got sick. This was after both boys, but Ben was just a baby. I'd done nursing, and after the milk wore away I still felt this nodule—thought it was a gland. Can you imagine a woman moving in on your family while you're half alive recovering from mastectomy?

"That must be the lowest of the low," she says.

But does Jelena think he's not going to repeat himself? I don't believe that any man's faithful.

"Tyler says I'm being ridiculous, crazy—says he's a writer, just following his nose."

Following his dick more likely.

"Don't you think that by fifty he'd begin to grow up?"

I don't believe you can mature somebody.

"Now he says he don't believe in vows. He broke 'em once with you, so what's the point of it."

I wonder why she wants to get married to him anyway. It's not like they're gonna have children.

"He says the one thing he likes about me, is how I always leave a toilet roll a paper on the back in case he runs out."

Well shit, I think, that *is* considerate.

We're both well aware that if he loved her enough he'd want to claim her for his bride and stop acting like a capon. Men are so sensitive about the state of their balls the illusion of freedom seems to be all they can care about.

"Some men can't handle commitment," I tell her, knowing it's that kind who can handle extra helpings of chicken pot pie.

I don't want my ex-husband to move to Lexington, remarry some trash and start another family. Jelena has been good to me, good to my children, but there's always going to be another Judith.

I try to explain it by way of his books. Tyler writes western romance, about two a year, and he needs to be in love with his characters, so he has to fabricate up this feeling out of life. Maybe he even loves his book people more than he loves his own folks, or maybe it's just his way of loving parts of himself.

"I don't care!" She stomps her rake and the chickens puff and scatter. "What about *me?*" A question I never asked myself.

I still want more info on Judith. I knew she was a heroine in one sequence of novels, long yellow hair and an excess in jewelry. She got her hair cut off now, well *haha*. Finally found some man who would marry her, but the baby pulled so hard on those long golden locks she had to buzz it right off, well too bad. I hope her husband's out screwing the sewing machine girl. Let her sit there with her baby and its donut-grip bottle.

"Oh yeah they were carryin' on," Jelena tells me, "while you was still recovering in the hospital. She wanted him to leave you — he wasn't ready for that."

I feel a sting in the dead flesh of my scar. This is my first confirmation.

"You know that woman, she sat at my table," I tell Jelena. "She held hands with my children and sang grace before the meal, said how it was such a nice family ritual."

"Well she'll fry in Hell," Jelena mutters, as if the chickens had ears. The dust from our rakes runs up along my arms but we're cooking now anyway.

"When I came home from Mount Mercy, she was there you know, to help with the boys, and I had to seem grateful — I guess I even was, but she was wearing one of Tyler's shirts as a nightgown — I'll never forget that, this blue an' green flannel shirt. She kinda saw my shock and came up with this concept — how she was gonna design a flannel dress sometime with fringe along the bottom, you could cinch at the waist? Sort of western style. She also thought up mid-calf jeans. Oh yeah, I said — the pedal pusher look. Next she'd be getting a ducktail. Wearing red bandana petty pants or something. But she acted like her ideas would all be news to me, and me there with a scar burning stitches across my chest, and she didn't even bother to wear a bra, just let her tits hang like insults."

"And *I'm* s'posed to be *nice* to this person?" Jelena asks me.

"You can shoot her along next to Tyler if you want to." I consider this Judith to be a water moccasin, and I just can't *breathe* when there's a snake in the vicinity.

I once told Tyler I thought she looked real cheap, and he said that could be a turn on. Well that felt good, one half of me missing and hearing that my man liked sleaze. "And that woman was walkin' my little baby!"

At the time I couldn't lift my arm. All I wanted was to sleep and let the world slide by. I didn't care if they went off to the movies after the kids went to bed, but sometimes I felt left, like an infant.

"At least you know what you're getting," I say to Jelena, no eighteen year old bride, banged up beforehand.

I think with Tyler I just always accepted. After the girls

grew up, we had these two boys, and whenever I was pregnant, I knew. I could smell it on him, as if the scent of her *stuck* till I named her perfume.

Now Jelena wants to know if the pattern will change.

"He'll come around," I say, meaning the wedding, as I drag the work basket over to the trash bin.

"But do I even *want* a man like that!"

I have no idea, but I suppose so. I want to say—It's none of my business. I don't envy most people their togetherness, always straining on each other. I feel all of a piece. Now my left arm can be used like the other one, and I've come to even like the angry feel of my scar, as if I'm half-man and half-woman, completed—I run this place like I am, anyhow.

My operation did ruin some things with Tyler. He was always what you'd call a "white meat man." I tried to get him focused on my rear end for instance, but he had this fixation and I couldn't switch that.

Jelena's well built, and I doubt this little typist could compete on that score. I just want to get even with Judith. Here's the thing—What got me thinking is that Judith's coming to town, bringing this big trunk of new designs. We small town gals are supposed to be impressed, wowed by her line a junk jewelry. Well Jelena and I are gonna try a couple of things on. Me and Jelena and a couple of our friends, we gonna squeeze our loving asses into some small-ass sizes and split 'em up the cheap-sewn seams! We laugh. And if she dares complain we gonna fucking wrap that stupid head a hers around the closest standing meter on Main.

"But listen now, honey," I say to Jelena. "You gotta figure if you really want him. If you do, you might as well settle on what you have, 'cause there ain't no changing nobody. And since I been alone, I ain't seen no man much different, so you can just stop examining phone bills."

93

"Well I want much more than half a nothing," she says, as if she's all done working and wants a drink a real coke. She is mad 'cause she can't plan her wedding, or pick out a dress.

"Hey, maybe you should get one a Judith's little numbers, tell her it's a gown to marry You-Know-Who. Tell her as if holding a gizzard knife, and maybe she'll consider a discount."

Maybe she'd like a chicken part crammed up her hind end, crawling down the runway with him in the audience. Maybe she'd like a wig to turn her rats nest head around so her face can go smother and we wouldn't have to look at her. Maybe she'd like a little barnyard style—right there in public, and he could participate.

Jelena and me, we be stomping in the front seat—*Sock-it-to-her, Sock-it-to-her, Sock-it-to-her, Sock-it-to-her,* then send this so-called woman home.

NOBODY LIKES THE RIGHT MAN

And I don't like the other ones either. I'm tired of their black snakes wriggling on the porch, men dropping like pick-up sticks around me. They are either pig-headed or inept without seasoning. I'm tired of their football mentality, telling me to squeeze tight my butt, and pretending to be a wave going uuuuUUUHHH! Crotch grabbing purse snatching — barrelling right at me, and then there's this tall blond following me around and a clown that wants to sit down next to me. I take back my hand. He makes nobody laugh, and the man who's supposed to be helping me — I don't even like *him*. You can take 'em in a bag and dump 'em over the side because they never were with me and certainly aren't for. Let them tell me I'm worth it some other year maybe, down in Barbados when I'm completely asleep, not listening to National Public Radio. Let life go on, for I'm shrinking away from it, becoming a more condensed individual, reducing, as they say, my own sauce. Other folks have people to look up to in their lives, while mine's been all made up. I am crushed when the characters refuse to participate. Well fine, let them write their own stories. Is there a right man for me, anywhere out there? Somehow I sincerely doubt it. I wouldn't know him if I saw him or I'd scare him away, and we wouldn't like each other, even if there was.

BULLIES & DUMMIES

My husband was a fucking bully if you want to know the truth. Tomorrow would have been our 20th, though I'm still under forty and he only hit me twice—there's more than one way to brutalize a woman.

So here I am, a *dee-vor-say,* disproving all those surveys. No available men? Will you give me a break. I don't say I got the best judgment, but then I don't like cold sheets.

First I took up with this part-time trucker. He had those little silver women on his back rubber tire guards. He said they looked a lot like me—plenty of hair and tons a tit, but then one night we were sitting in this restaurant, and he puts his big ugly mitt on my boob and says, "I don't want you looking up at other guys. And don't talk back." I might be kind a small but I am *not* defenseless. I took my glass a water and dumped it on his head. I coulda sworn he took sprout and was like some maniac bull buck in killer uniform. These dicks don't know where to get off.

So I went in the opposite direction for a while, fell in with someone "artistic," but I think he was *bi,* and in this day-and-age you gotta put yourself on the dummy list. I wasn't sure till we were in the sack, and then he wanted me to *talk,* to help him out and shit. I don't mind things getting raunchy if it's physical and hot, but I don't like to *think* when I'm doin' it.

Men are really out to save their own hides, I swear. It's the women who are taking all the risks. Some guys protect themselves with Work—there's a favorite—they accuse you of being a distraction, *sore-ree,* and make you pay for it plenty— all the money they might have lost while out seeing you. Sports is another way of hiding.

The next guy was over-weight but awful adoring—he

really put the rush on me, but as soon as I started to warm up to him, *flick,* he was out of there, invisible.

Sometimes you feel like you can do no right. I've had bruisers get hysterical if I smear a little chrome. Well some folks eat chicken with their hands, OK? That's the way we always did it, southern fried, back home — you gnaw on those drumsticks, none of this *nouvelle cuisine* shit.

I like things spicey and I drink hard booze. I like to get loose on the dance floor — *Yo* — unless I'm with a bully like that one who was yanking me around, then squeezed me till I gasped, "That hurts!" He kept saying how he liked his girls hard. I said, "Women are supposed to be soft, you dummy." He kissed with a vengeance, all that softness I guess reminded him of something he wanted to crush.

Too many of these guys are working things out in the bedroom that still belong on the football field. Recently I dreamt a whole bunch of 'em were playing with a loaf of mouldy bread. The staff of life, gone green and putrid. My God, every slice needed to be sent back, way before I even dreamt that.

Women aren't meant for punting, jerks, but men consider my chest fair field. Guys can not get over it when you take off your shirt and unhook — they go nuts — and you begin to feel your true power over them. They turn into the biggest dummies you ever saw, little babies wanting sugar tit mammie — I swear it brings up all kinds of garbage.

Some men can't handle excitement and their tools turn mean. This one guy had to fuck me till I bled, real nice. He made me suck on his fingers while he told me what a cunt I was, how spoiled fucking rotten — I swear. I guess I can live without that.

I keep dreaming about this injured boy, carried off on a stretcher, the rodeo too rough. I want to comfort and protect him. I want to find out the asshole who did this shit. I have always been a hell-bitch on wheels, even as a kid, no holding me back — like that time I lit into

Roxie Renny over that label on the Hawaiian Punch.

My primary school was some education. First came Mrs. Voltz. Stick your finger in that. Then Mrs. Bolton. She can speak for herself. Miss Dentice was like a drill, believe. Mrs. Weston made me wash Ash Wednesday off after the priest said to let it wear. Mrs. Bumby made me cry because she couldn't teach math. I wept every day in the girls' room, looking for pictures in the marbelized tile. Miss Lemon was the crowning blow. She swore I'd never go to college. So I married out of high school thanks to her.

Perhaps there is no such thing as normal. No one has a normal childhood for instance. My father was a bully. He used to spank my ass. I have a good meaty butt and I think he liked the sound of impact, flesh smacking flesh, and the struggle I put up, him yanking down my drawers, just because Deedee and I made too much noise while he was trying to boff our step-mom. I would turn myself around and check his hand print in the mirror, blubbering for full effect. "Those girls are just wearing me out," I'd hear her say. I could have punched in her face for being such a fat head.

I never told what my step-brothers did to me. One time when she was out, they chased me around the house, pinned me down, then pulled up my t-shirt and rubbed deodorant on my pits. They said if I screamed they would have to break me in, and they held up this Schlitz beer bottle. I thought they meant to break it inside a me, and my fuckin' nails *grew*. I said — My father's gonna kill! But they said he'd be happy to watch it, and when I started to cry they got out their whangers and peed on my crotch. They said I must have wet my little undies, and if I ever told they'd rope me to a tree and tie real live snakes around my ankles.

So life goes on, but you kinda drag it with you. I think of those guys and picture animal carnage. But it's strange how they got me turned on to this stuff — how I almost came to think

I wanted it. When I got a little older, I was really built, and they'd get me in the basement and play stink finger with me. They told me about the 4 F Club: Find 'em, Feel 'em, Fuck 'em and Forget 'em. They said someday I'd beg to kiss their little worms. *Right,* I thought, *whatever.*

Not too long ago I was seeing this one guy who was kind of nice, but complacent as a summer stump. On beer. He wanted to use me without using any energy, and that passive aggressive shit's the worst, you know? He liked me to sit across the room from him and play with myself, as if he had remote control.

One cute fella said his cars came first, but his head was still back with the cub scouts. He thought he'd get a badge I guess for each new position — on the trunk of the Porsche, hood of the Mercedes, then the gear shift of the Maserati. This can get tiresome. With the damn calendar on the wall. They want you to act like Miss January.

So now I dream of looking in the water and see a load of dead fish. I ask my father why they died, something poisoning the water? I think maybe it's my real mother's booze problem. Maybe I inherited the poison from her, her willingness to take it and go under.

I'm just afraid for that boy, the one who slips out the backdoor and is seen in the sun on his bicycle, golden. He is just too good, almost feminine — gone. Maybe he'll grow up to be a man who could save me, a man without a dummy smile, and six reasons why I should ride in his 4 x 4, a man who's not eager to grip my wrist so hard the blood stops, a man who doesn't fantasize of sitting me in a pan of raw liver, or of taking another man in front of me.

I know in many ways I'm responsible. I've been bullied worst by my own stinking love, how easily and often it's tricked me, made me fall for another wrong guy. I've got to talk real sense to my love now, for we're only given so many pearls, and I've been tossing mine out before swine.

Last night I had a dream about these "lovers" in my past. They were stuffed and jiggling above this empty counter, as if they were all plugged in, Howdy Doody type cowboys with stuffed straw forms, a line-up of your basic dummies. Outside the restaurant there was a filling station, selling gas for only 2¢. I say — Hey, that's pretty cheap, I bet they get all the business.

So maybe I have been kind of cheap also, with too many customers, but believe-you-me, these rates are going up. You might think I'm just a mega-bitch who had it hard coming, but I'm not so different than your mother. Blame her! Go on, jack off with your excuses. Even if you could you wouldn't want to remember. Ever think why she wore sunglasses *inside* the house?

I think about speaking from the belly, sticking a hand up the backside of a dummy and bringing him to life — how I've tried to get these puppets to perform for me, and when they don't say the words I thought I had coming — I toss a fresh sack of bones along the road.

But I no longer want to make anybody pay. I am all worn out, dead tired. Sick of pleasing men and expecting something in return. I want to believe there is hope as well as hurting. It's my life now and I'm gonna fucking water it. I'm gonna sit here till I see a flower grow.

So this morning before waking I dreamt this mountain pool. I am gazing down deep, then see this stag in the water — he's got the most beautiful full rack you ever seen, but I can't look up — I'm afraid I might lose him. Then the sun shifts, and I see that it's a man. He can tell how I'm feeling — all alone in this world. I think he is thinking — Poor cookie, little girl — you're afraid of being loved, you just never trusted anyone. He says this without even speaking to me, and I know him somehow without ever having known. It feels good just to be there in his presence. His eyes say—Gentle, no hurry, here. He holds out his hand, and I want to say, *Help me*—It's the damnedest hardest thing I've ever had to do—but with all of my might—I reach for it.

I TOLD YOU I WAS SICK

Tonight it must be close to eighty degrees and I only need this light sheet over me, the ceiling fan humming above. A gentle splash from the fountain sounds below in the garden of the Villa Bougainvillea, a 50's motel resurrection, in spicy peach stucco with turquoise trim. The voluptuous garden is central to the rooms, with gargantuan fern and fruit trees, orchids hung in planters and something sweet — an aromatic mock orange.

I unscrew the lightbulb every night in my art nouveau fixture, just outside. I'm not used to the glare, but the manager is a little fussy, and comes behind me, rescrewing. The lights give the walkway a spatial effect, and he is also affected. He looks like he's aspiring to be a French bicyclist who'd rather not race today.

I haven't been concerned about picking up guys. Here in Key West, they're picking up each other, and I'm glad to have the company of my son. I'm the one who always takes him on vacation. His father has a girl friend now.

I don't want to consider my son a partner, not even a replacement. When I think of sex, I don't think of him anymore than I think of my own arm.

But have you ever tried making love to yourself in absolute silence, because your small son's asleep in the same room? Life in this tropical climate, with the constant warmth and lingering smart of sunburned skin, makes me long for climax.

Just this afternoon, Chiqui lay on his own queen-size bed batting the tent-pole of his little erection.

What a pair, I thought.

"I hate it when people think I'm a girl," he announced.

"I suppose you should take it as a compliment," I said. "Because you're so cute."

"Still," he said. He is intensely blond with delicate features. His hair curls over his ears and hangs low on his forehead. Even as a baby, people often mistook him for a female child.

He sleeps now naked from the waist down in a neon, peach shade t-shirt that makes his tan seem caramel. He is a delicious boy.

I am in love with Morgan Thompson, my professor of marine biology. Now that my course is over, we're writing each other postcards. There's been some stir on campus, teachers involved with young students, and he thought it best if we waited a while before making a public friendship. He's recovering from someone else anyway.

This postcard pictures Hemingway's House, one of the main attractions: *No need for sweaters here, smells of jasmine like honey pouring out the spout, my mood a melting curve. The seas are a buoyant azure, the coral reefs alive, angelfish and snorkelers approaching an inner blue.*

It's amazing how orgasms vary for me. Sometimes it's just like pushing a cotton ball over the edge of a canyon, but sometimes it's like threading the juicy taut stems of flower stalks tight till they bloom. Sometimes it's like digging a tunnel through sand that suddenly collapses, and sometimes it's like a small wave washing out the name of some man. So many have come and faded.

It was exciting for me to go back to school, but then to have this tall, handsome professor, who even looked good in glasses, and there were all these adoring girls, while he appeared — Well, almost noble.

My love for this man wasn't just a love for his person, but more like a longing for the depths. The younger girl students didn't interest him, he said, but still he had to be on guard. One of his colleagues had just lost his job, and Morgan was a single man.

"You're the first guest to even *ask* about Tennessee Williams," the manager tells me. It is clear he has no one to talk to, and I'm afraid if I linger for directions I'll get stuck. Outside the light is dazzling. My son comes to stand in the doorway, slurping an overripe star fruit. It smells of drenched edible flowers. We have rented a scooter to ride around town. Today is Valentine's Day.

I remember the card my ex-husband gave me four years ago. Only now it touches me. At the time I was too resolved. It was simply a picture of Lassie. He'd drawn a big red heart on her chest.

When our son was born ten years ago, we called him, "Chiquitito." He was so small and cute, five pounds, seven ounces, and every time I said that word, it was like holding a wren in two hands, hunching up with protectiveness. "Chiqui," we say for short.

I sent Morgan Thompson a heart-shaped candle: *Keep Your Love Light Lit.* Sometimes I feel a little foolish, knowing he's recovering from this married woman who will not leave her husband, who will not leave her home. Someday he'll get over it.

Chiqui complains that his hair is in his eyes. I get out the scissors from my travelling bag and almost before he knows what's happening, I hold up the front locks and snip. A solid inch of blond silk falls into the black basin. He bursts into tears, "I didn't mean so much!"

I say I'm sorry, but I'm really not. He's being vain. And sorrow doesn't suit him. His nose is peeling and his shorts are a neon pink, matching the flaming flamingo pressed onto the neon peach.

When he hears his friends outside on the patio, two younger boys from room 17, he forgets his tribulations. I will take my afternoon shower splash, then read in the nude on my balcony, where the bougainvillea streams in strands of shocking cerise tangled in with a tawny orange. It hides me from the other patrons, but not from the afternoon sun.

I like getting to that point in a vacation when I don't have to plan every moment—I can trust that things will unfold. Reaching for a ripened mango, I eat right down to the pit, so big and slimy with sweet meat. The gentleness of the air makes me feel a deep contentment. I'm glad to hear the children playing, running around the upper walkway, until the voice of the manager, "Hey! NO RUNNING!"

I can hear my son say, "Why can't we run?"

"Because I SAID SO and if you do it again I'll call the police, OK?" There is a stunned silence. I picture a bunch of juicy fresh flowers, crushed, leaving a stain on the grey cement.

I talk to the children's mother, Diana. "If everything else weren't booked," she says, "we could hang out someplace else. But don't let it ruin your vacation. He's just an unhappy man."

She is lovely, exuberant, with thick brown hair and a freckled face that isn't taking a tan well. "It's great the boys found each other," I say. "Maybe if we make ourselves scarce. Why don't we rent a fishing boat?"

The next morning we board *The Illusion,* and our skipper, Jim, is short and quick, exceptionally nice to the children. The boys sit in back as we roar out of the harbor to where the gulf is connected to the ocean by a tidal stream that pulls back and forth with big schools of fish.

As the boat flies out onto open water, we talk. She is presently getting a divorce. "I can't tell you how great I feel," she says. "Though everybody thinks I'm an idiot." Her husband is handsome, successful, fit, and boring her to death.

Jim anchors the boat near a sandy shoal, and as soon as the hooks are loaded, they begin pulling in one after another— snapper, grouper, grunt.

Diana talks on about her husband, more quietly now, and a hook of red herring wags between our faces. "Watch it guys!" We get them oriented toward the back of the boat. The sun off the water is intense. "He's the kind of man," she whispers, "who has seven suits, and he rotates them exactly so they won't wear out."

I tell her about Morgan Thompson, how great it was being back in school, going on field trips together, identifying various wildlife in the wetlands. "I decided to quit because of the student-teacher conflict," I say. "I just have to be a little patient." I tell her how I invited him over for dinner and he said — Let's just wait a little bit longer.

"That sounds encouraging," she agrees. But when she learns that he's forty-five and never been married, never had a child of his own, she adds, "Sounds like high risk material."

"I got one. I got it!" A long pole bends, and her older son reels in a snapper. Jim unhooks the fish, measures it, then throws it in the cooler, alive.

"My husband's dating this lawyer," she says. "Every weekend she flies up from Washington, and his mother's all excited."

"He'll probably marry the first woman he sees. That's what mine's doing. You'd better be prepared."

"These snapper got to be twelve inches now," Jim complains. "I tell you it's ridiculous." He believes it's all a cover-up for the bigger issues, like what commercial fishermen are doing to the dolphin in order to catch high-priced tuna. They round the dolphin up with helicopters, catch them in nets, where they often smother, or they're slaughtered later, thousands and thousands of those intelligent creatures, mammals, just like us.

I promised myself I wouldn't talk about it, but I feel I can confide in Diane, for who do we know in common. So I tell her about the first time Morgan Thompson kissed me. He was afraid of losing his job.

I had come into his office after a late night class to discuss my proposal for independent study, a project concerning the migration of local, spotted salamander, and right before I left we were both standing up, and oh yes, it was almost his birthday, because I'd bought him this record of whale songs and he seemed extremely touched, as if no one else had remembered. I think he was depressed about that woman professor, and then he opened his arms and we kissed, which to me felt like sinking in water, dying an irresistible death, out of myself—gone into him. I didn't think there was anything wrong. We were both consenting adults. But for a moment I felt the butane of a tiny anger licking at the base of my neck. I wanted Morgan Thompson to forget her.

"Help," her younger son yells. "Here it comes!" He can barely hang onto the fish as it shoots back and forth, diving under the boat.

"Looks like a shark," Jim says, peering. Nothing we'll want to keep. But he grabs it out of the water, shows us its evil hammerhead, the cup-shaped mouth and pure white belly.

"Lots of man-of-war right now. Gotta watch these kids if you go swimming." We had seen their bloated bodies on the shore like condoms of the sea. "Surf's all stirred up," Jim adds. "That's why we didn't go deep today." He tells us how man-of-war can dangle their acid hot tentacles across the back of your neck, how a sting can confuse even a good swimmer.

Chiqui catches a fourteen incher, and I snap his picture with the disposable camera roll I bought in Key Largo, then take a turn at the rod myself. Jim puts a small squid on my hook and shows me how to cast, but I only get an ugly Warsaw grouper in army fatigue, too small, while Diana spots a school of transparent jellyfish and wants to scoop one out.

"No way," Jim warns. "Even when they're dead they'll sting ya."

Back on the pier, Jim filets all eighteen fish, while the kids dance around taking turns throwing refuse to the crowd of pelicans that has gathered on the dock of Garrison Bite. "Watch out," I say. "Don't tease them."

The restaurant on the pier cooks the filets up for us—

baked, fried, blackened. We order beer and Diane admires the way the fish are presented, like circular rays around the cut-open lemon.

"You should check out The Everglades when you go back," I suggest. "Don't you think our guide was a little weird though?"

Chiqui agrees. "He wouldn't even let us eat lunch!" Food has become a major preoccupation.

But at least he knew his marsh mythology, sort of a Cajun type, Leroy Saltete. The Cadillac engine in his airboat was so loud we had to use ear plugs, but still the vibration tickled my eardrums as we charged up and down these long marshy lanes — over masses of lilypad flowers, gators sunning on the banks or twisting away, the phantom forms of heron lifting off beyond.

"And then he put this raw liver on a hook and caught a baby alligator and handed it to me," I tell the whole table. Diane goes *ugh*. "It was actually much softer than you'd think, more like a lizard."

"Please," she says.

But Leroy had more information than even I cared to hear. "They tell you a 'gator can live seventy years, but I tell you I saw one as wide as this boat, must have been a twenty footer. A four year old girl just got eaten," he said. "They cut her right outa its belly."

"Was she alive?" my son asked, a reader of fairy tales.

The marsh smell of mud and honeysuckle seemed to mix together and I felt nauseous from the heat of the sun. "Did you know a 'gator's faster in the first thirty feet than the fastest racehorse alive?"

"I don't believe that," my son said to me later, though I could imagine it with those buzz-saw legs.

He lifted the flap that was the baby alligator's ear, showed us that it was a male, stroking the valuable leather of the belly while speaking of the tanning process.

Then he wanted to lead us to an alligator cave, way out on this spongy tundra.

Walking along the path, I wondered, "What's going to keep *this* alligator from attacking us?"

"Well this here sow, she's only eight foot. She'd have to be ten to mess with a human. She's got sensors all over her body," he said. "She could tell if we were just a ten pound raccoon, or tiny deer," then — *boom.*

The animals came to drink and die at her watering hole, the food chain as vicious as the love chain. I knew I was a charm on the chain of fools, but still it kept me going.

We began to meet regularly the last three weeks of the semester. At the end of class he would give me this look and I'd head on over to his office. It was dark and he always left the door unlocked. We were getting more familiar and he said things like, "You know this won't affect your grade." His kisses and hands were like a whirlpool I sank into. "I can't wait for this semester to be over," he said. He couldn't see me socially until then.

My girlfriend back home gave me a hand-painted valentine of a heart submerged in the depths of black water. It made me feel a little lonely to look at it. My ex-husband sent me a card of two hunters shooting Cupid right out of the air. I gave our son a postcard of puppies, stuck a decal of a heart on one chest and wrote: *Are you the sweetest in the bunch?* For he was the son of Lassie.

Captain Leroy pulled up a jagged blade of saw grass so that Chiqui could chew on the tasteless tip. "That'll keep you alive if you get stuck out there." I could almost taste the milky goodness of the crabmeat sandwich I had waiting in the cooler on the airboat.

He flicked at a mud nest built up in the bushes, said, "Fire ants, see? We kids used to rub these on each other and run. Guess you can imagine what that feels like." He smiled my way, and I ran my hands up onto the heat of my shoulders. I knew that pain, like sunburn, could stimulate the body, make it tender, more responsive to the touch.

Finally back at the boat he let us feed, while he pelted an alligator with marshmallows—its hard snout drifted by, opening to *chomp* that sweetness, nictitating membranes descended over black, lidless eyes.

By the time we got back on the road it was dusk, and we drove across this long stretch of agricultural land—summery, humid, verdant. As it got darker, sprinklers started shooting powerful spray that pummelled the car. We passed one field and there were bright lights shining down, as if to force the crop's production. A community of bare white trailers stood behind a wire fence, and I wondered if they were for people, no windows to be seen, but then I saw baby clothes hanging on a line, a pick-up truck loaded with workers, and I was filled with a longing for the world, for the earthy sadness of these fields.

When we got to Key Largo that night, we could hear reggae music from our hotel room, black men with bongos, a sweet rhythm in their bodies that never seemed to quit. The sunshine, now gone, was still making me hot, and I remembered other Valentine Days, like different forms of disappointment.

First there was the man who helped break up my marriage. I went to New York to be with him, and he left me alone in his apartment to go out to a black-tie dinner. He was needed as an extra bachelor. When he returned he brought me a Hallmark card. The next year, I was given a blue box from Tiffany's, but the silver heart wasn't even from there, I checked. A year later the man I was dating tossed a brown paper bag across the bed. It held a stretchy red sex suit that I could barely touch. He admitted he preferred to see me naked, but got offended when I cashed it in.

If I were a guy I'd know the meaning of roses, of real silk lingerie.

"But you got to let them know you *need* them," Diane says. "You look like you don't need anyone. I love to use my femininity." She has pinned up her hair and it's tumbling down. Her emerald, sandwashed t-shirt is slipping off one shoulder.

I lick the stamp for Morgan's postcard, which pictures the Seven Mile Bridge: *We sailed on a boat called Illusion, but still caught real live fish. Grouper in garlic butter for luncheon. Delicious continual indulgence. I only shudder when I see TV reporters shouting through the snow. Is it possible we really live there? Meanwhile the sun plugs this place as the best. Hope Cupid was good to you.*

Diane wants to take a sunset champagne cruise on a huge pontoon boat. I'm game. The boys can drink unlimited sodas which breaks our rule—just one a day. "But this is vacation, Mom!"

Diane assesses the men on board. "I've got a good eye," she says, picking out a member of the crew, a tall blond with a very dark tan. I wonder if he's bi-sexual.

A man with a gold chain and a huge pot belly tries to start a conversation about real estate in Miami, but then the one she noticed comes around to pour us all champagne. He gives me a look which digs in.

"I think you've been getting too much sun," I tease him. He is from Amsterdam and yes, appealing. "But he's probably only twenty-five," I whisper.

"So what!" And we both start laughing, glad to be out on the water, sitting on the tarp stretched floor of the boat.

The guy comes around to pour us some more and puts his hand on my shoulder. Each time he circles he is more attractive, a little closer to arousing a flirtation. He wants to sell me a t-shirt of the boat and I say, "I like the one you have on," plucking the material.

I have worn my tight white matador pants and now that the sun has gone down, I feel free to gently sway with the music, swinging my son by the elbow.

"I think he likes you, Mom," Chiqui tells me. He is discreet, unlike Diane's children, who are yelling, "Let's invite him for dinner!" We've got plenty of food, and I say,

"Go ahead," but at the last moment she chickens out.

We eat by ourselves on the open air patio of the Villa Bougainvillea, under the spotlight I will later unscrew. We are feeling a bit deflated, "Oh well," feasting on French bread, tomatoes, arugola, blush wine, fried local shrimp and broccoli.

For a moment Morgan Thompson is forgotten. I haven't slept with anyone since I fell in love with him, though once another student had a crush on me and Morgan even called me "fickle." The air in his office went electric that night. I had to stop him from doing something he might regret. "Let's wait," I said, sitting up on the sofa, smoothing out the material of my dress.

He told me he was spending the summer at Woods Hole. His invitations were never clear or direct. I said my feet were too freezing to even think about summer, so he pulled off my boots and felt my stocking covered feet. He said, "I'd love to see your body in a wet suit."

I pick up the book I've been reading to Chiqui, "*I am glad we do not have to kill the stars,*" but he wants to go down to the swimming pool, where the kids are batting a beach ball back and forth.

I feel like all anxiety has dropped from my shoulders like a robe to the floor. It's been unseasonably mild, and I haven't had to wear a sweater all week. I think of Morgan Thompson, and the image of him feels so close and warm, the way the weather feels to my skin right now — constant, caressing, gentle.

I like what I see in the mirror. My good, bare breasts are neither small nor large, but high and round and firm, a sanding of crushed coral and salt on my chest, left from my morning swim. I don't like the chlorine and the kids are afraid of the undertow. I pull on a tight white t-shirt and the shape of my breasts shines through. My teeth appear bright against the orangey-bronze lipstick. There are sensors all over my body.

Just then I hear the manager yelling by the pool, "I told YOU yesterday to COOL it or you're OUT OF HERE!" He is shaking his fist at my son, who presently creeps into our motel room, dripping.

"We weren't doing *anything*," he protests. "What a tool."

"We'll just have to keep a low profile," I tell him, "and when we get home, I'll write the Chamber of Commerce."

Later that afternoon, walking down Duval Street, we dip through the plastic bands that seal a store from the fumes of the street and are momentarily overwhelmed by perfume. The man behind the counter is wearing a diamond engagement ring, and has the tiniest of grey toy poodles, "Sevier."

I ask him if he has any Tuber Rose and he holds up a card and sprays like a painter. "Try this," he says. "A lot of people like this Tea Rose. You can spray it on a lightbulb, a cold lightbulb," he corrects himself, "and when it warms, it's like the room is filled with flowers."

Out on the street I smell the card and like it. It really does smell like roses. "Would you wear this?" I ask my son.

"I don't wear perfume, remember — I'm a boy. That dog's dick was out the whole time."

"It was?" The street has a carnival aroma, Cuban food, people in the late afternoon sunshine still cruising this southern-most tip of America, *I Went All the Way, KEY WEST*, women wearing strapless, colorful bra bands, and my son checks out a hat he thinks he might buy for his Dad. It has a set of tits above the brim. There are postcards of gay guys with swim-suit erections, unconcealed asses of some perfectly tanned butts. We stop in at the Key Oasis Resort, and I ask the magazine vendor for the ladies' room. "There's a pile of sand over in the corner," he says.

Out on the pier, jugglers, cartoonists and a tightrope walker entertain the crowded pack. They are primed to see the sun go down, to cheer in boozy elation. Just as the sun hits the edge of the horizon, a sword swallower thrusts a blade down his throat. I feel no particular need to rejoice, no need for despair—I am only like the lulling of the warm salt waters, the surface of glittery light, holding the form of one man in my mind, as if he were floating in my element.

In general I believe women are more shallow when it comes to relationship. Men get attached at a deeper level, and when a love affair's over, they are ripped apart by some invisible cord that goes right up the middle—it's almost like gutting a fish. But if a woman can stand to get the hook out, she's bound to flip over the edge, disappearing in translucent waters. Losing a child is the one thing that could destroy us.

My son pulls a crunched-up valentine from his pocket, and reads it over to himself. I can see it says: *Dear Chiqui, I love you very, very much.* I like her sense of repetition, and ask him, "Who's it from?"

At first he doesn't want to tell me, but then confesses, "She's a grade above," giving me her initials. I approve of her and her directness, even if it doesn't work with adult men.

Another girl came up to my son on the playground, and said, "I don't like her. She shouldn't get somebody like you."

"Sounds like jealousy to me," I instruct him, though I'm also vaguely jealous of the flame-colored hair of the pregnant professor. I try not to think about that.

Sometimes I think I frighten Morgan Thompson, by being too available or real. It's like the difference between seeing a fish behind glass and actually holding one in your hands.

The last week of the semester, I broke down and cried, saying I didn't think he'd want to go forward, that he wouldn't have the time or inclination. He shook his head in disbelief.

As we say goodbye to our new friends, we promise to get back together, maybe on vacation next year. We are heading

115

for the Dolphin Research Center near Islamorada, where we'll get to swim with the dolphins, the one thing Chiqui really wanted to do.

The rubbery smooth skin of the dolphins feels slick, and their chittering talk is adorable. I'm amazed by the feel of their bodies. They wag their bottle noses, confident that their trainer will reward them after every dorsal fin ride. Then they zoom through the water in unison, leaping up like animated joy.

At noon we are just in time to catch the boat to the coral reef. The waves were too high earlier in the trip, and our flight doesn't leave till seven.

They give us inflatable vests, which keep us feeling weightless. With fins and masks, hand in hand, we let the water float our limbs as the fish swim below us, the saline lift and steady inhalation, so easy as we wag around the giant brain coral we've been instructed not to touch, sea fans waving as the fish circle round it, little spurts of several dart then drift in outrageous blue, green, yellow. A few barracuda lurk down by the bottom. They do look sinister, but supposedly won't hurt. Chiqui is easily chilled.

He squeezes my hand and points back to the boat. I hate to leave this world of underwater — the visibility great today. A bright blue angelfish swims by, staghorn and starlet coral. We crawl up the plank like creatures, shower in the open air of the boat. I tell him to rest in the sun now, to soak up these last few hours.

Our flight departs on schedule. I'm all worn out, want to sit and read. Chiqui compares our tans, same golden brown, my arm to his. I persuade him to leave me alone.

We have to change planes in Chicago, and smokers have filled the terminal with excess smoke. I can feel it weave into my hair, my clothes. I resent this change in weather. "Different attitudes for different latitudes," my son sings, repeating some lyrics he heard in Key Largo.

Finally on the last flight toward Minneapolis, Chiqui falls

116

asleep. Then the pilot announces there's a blizzard down below, and they might fly us back to Chicago. The entire plane groans in unison, but as we descend, the plane seems to shiver. I wonder if I'll receive any correspondence at home.

Morgan usually answers my postcards promptly, and always has something sweet and witty to say. The pilot breaks in and says we're in line now for landing. I look at my son's sleeping face. Suddenly he sits up, damp with sleep and confused, as the lights down below show the blizzard flying straight at us. I can feel the strain on the wings, bending to the force of the storm. We approach the white, glazed field, then jolt— screeching to an extended stop. The entire plane claps and cheers. But look at this disgusting weather.

We still have to drive another forty minutes home, peering through the windshield, stopping every ten minutes to de-ice the wipers. Even with four-wheel drive, I still swivel on the ungroomed highway.

Usually I'm so glad to get home. I always say it's the best part of the trip, but now I feel a chill between my wingbones, holding the letter I'd expected. My son staggers up to bed and I tell him, "Sleep, my love, sleep in."

I go into the bathroom and read: *Your postcards have been warmly received, quite wonderful, and I hope to keep our correspondence alive, but now, as I think of it, I'm tentative in connecting any more with you. It's a complicated time in my career. I don't think a romance would be favored by the stars, but I do hope you're fine and that your trip went well.*

I am just too tired for this. What might have been the icing on the cake becomes the frosting on the storm. I am even too tired to sleep. I lie in bed and think cold thoughts— *Charlatan, Faggot, Acid, Liar*—like spurts of squid ink darkening the night.

It strikes me that even the ugliest, meanest, most loathsome people seem to secure a mate. Sometimes I feel like one of those fish that swims at the very bottom of the ocean, in utter darkness, with brilliant colors no one can perceive. Perhaps I would ache less if I could only achieve a state of passionate indifference. Or is there such a thing as beauty, unbeheld, true love, without a willing partner.

CHALK ONE UP

Really, I don't care anymore — whether I have splatter spots on my sweat pants, or if my gut gets progressively fat. I've stopped making the bed and crawl into the covers littered with towels and books. I don't change when I get up in the morning, and pull — whatever, from the oven each night. I don't even set the table. Why bother. All the light has been ripped from my iris. It doesn't matter if I go out or stay in. Strange not to have expectations. I am bleeding, but I make no effort to catch it. So what if it splashes my ankles or the rug. If I were an animal I might keep myself clean, but now if I break something, I just step over it. I can take any outfit from the pile. I see no reason to put all of this away. I don't linger over anything. I can't savor anymore. I don't notice very much as I walk out to the car. I don't plan or look forward to anything. There seems to be no urgency in my path anymore. I don't speed and my mail has lost interest. I have cared so much I don't care anymore. Driving home, I see an animal on the roadside. It appears to be an orange and white cat, with its guts stretched out from a gash in its belly. But the animal doesn't even seem to notice. Licking its own left paw.

HOW NOT TO SEDUCE YOUR THERAPIST

Why don't you come visit my house," I suggest. "Someday when I'm not there."

I know my therapist has a penchant for peeping, why else would he have chosen this profession. And now he's got a real live opportunity. He wonders what's behind all this.

"Don't you think a house can be an extension of the soul? Don't you think you'd find out more about me than I could tell you in a hundred sessions?"

My little white house is set like a jewel at an angle, catching the afternoon sun. I have left the place clean, but not overly tidy. The windows have been washed which lends a luminous quality. As he enters, he is drawn through numerous intimate rooms, which seem to unfold one after another, each in some surprising and pleasing shade. Paintings appear like unexpected flowers and there's a window seat comfortable with cushions.

He finds himself standing in the yellow slant of the kitchen, surrounded by the smell of sugar and cinnamon I've sprinkled in the oven, giving the illusion that he has finally come home. A generous bunch of peonies is displayed on the dining room table, twelve deflowered princesses with red flecks on their gowns.

He walks down the stairs into the peach-colored piano room that remains light and cool even in the summer. The tone of the piano is magical. Any song he thinks of he can play. An open bottle of Merlot is breathing there, and he takes some in the goblet that's been provided for this purpose. It puts him in the mood for love, longing for some hidden partner.

Upstairs he knows how Goldilocks must have felt, though everything feels "just right" here. He could sink forever in that featherbed—the smell of overripe fruit rises from the depths of the unmade linens, and the lingerie drawer has been partly left open. I have encouraged him to go through my things.

Turning to go, he hears the trickle of the stream that lulls me to sleep each evening. It feeds into a pond that fills and overflows, just as the two of us would do, wrapped in the music of the junipers.

He is feeling light-headed, but must still see my study, the smallest and furthest room in the house. As he enters, I feel like he's taking possession of my body, even though I'm nowhere around, or perhaps, in my house, I am indeed ever-present. He touches the smooth dark wood of my writing desk, and reads the message I have left for him there.

He looks up, as if stunned, and sees the bench out the window, surrounded by jack-in-the-pulpit. Someday he would like to wander on that path—he can already feel himself falling. Everything is just too good, and it makes him incredibly sleepy. He walks out into the garden and lies down in the hammock, feeling utterly at peace as the tanagers sing and the deep purple lilacs spill down.

His head now is filled and he dozes for a moment, dreaming of a golden mare. But she rears and she twists as if to overpower him—the horse's furry muzzle is kissing him on the mouth, and he feels like a black rubber bucket, licked clean. When he wakes I am glaring down at him.

I tell him that his hour was up long ago. It comes out that I hate all men. Now my therapist is no better than the worst kind of woman. Love and passion have been my disguise.

"Why are you doing this?" my therapist asks me.

"Because!" I say. "I'm revenging my mother." I say. Like some tattered Cinderella doing her dirty work. Suddenly her dark cloak falls.

My eyes become coals that could burn the whole house down. The rip of a chainsaw is roaring in my throat, and this bilious black lava shoots out. It is wretched, I'm awful, so reduced here and helpless, vomiting up this sickening dead snake, until only a liquid like sea water leaves me and a little orange goldfish swims out.

Now I'm at peace and myself again. When I open my eyes, he is stroking my hair, for I am his daughter, his sister, his own dying mother, the wife that he wanted but lost, all the children that desired to be born in his name and which still fill his life with longing.

I would marry him today and make the world fit togther, but I know that that is not for me to say. So I leave, leaving that warm, empty space in his arms, like the place where a deer lies down in the tall grass, coming back every night to peer into his dream, looking in the moonlight for herself.

PART THREE

ANIMALS IN LOVE

I was originally going to call this *Always In Love*, because Socrates and I are like-minded. He once said, "I can't think of a time in my life when I wasn't in love." Not very bright of us, granted.

But what's wisdom got to do with spring? Young girls fall in love for the pleasure of the gallop, first this sorrel and then some little bay. Love, like a grass fire racing over the surface while the male of the species is more reluctant.

He's not used to getting hurt monthly, so he doesn't bounce back—high across the springtime fields. I want a stream to leap and a son to go with it—Ayler on his little black Star.

I rode by his side on Cody, a tawny gold horse whose canter's so slow it's delicious. Poor little Star fell in love with him. They were together in the pasture five days, and when I had to ride Cody home again, we could hear her whinnying for miles.

Several times he stopped along the road, dead still, as if to say—I'm not going further without her. But it doesn't take much to make a man move on. When I returned, Star looked desolate in the field.

Mango, the chow pup, tried to make her feel better, and kept dangling around like some hopeful friend. I clipped the long red lead onto Star's blue halter, gave her a hug and led her into the backyard where there's juicy green grass to graze upon.

Then while I cleaned the basement windows (the better not to see you with, my love), Mango picked up the red lead in her mouth and pulled the pony around the yard.

WHY I NO LONGER SEND POSTCARDS

This one, picturing a man looking under his armpit, peeking into an empty shoe, and then down his own pants, is captioned: *Looking for love in all the wrong places,* and I'm headed for Arizona.

Rick wasn't sure about a long-distance romance, but I rather liked keeping in touch through postcards. You can say a whole lot in such a small space. You can give yourself over to longing without having to do extra laundry.

Rick said that he would fly me out there, but couldn't see me again all summer.

I decided to send him a postcard of a paranoid steer: *I just found out how they make hamburger!* Another cow answers: *You leftists and your conspiracy theories. Get a grip on yourself, honey!*

I wrote him that I wasn't comfortable with such a long separation and couldn't he come up with a solution?

He answered that he didn't want to talk about it. We'd have to take one trip at a time.

I dreamt I took my eight year old son to his ranch and neither of us was welcome. There was another woman sitting at Rick's table. I turned to my son and said to him, "This is why they call it the desert, because there's nothing for us here."

I sent Rick one last minute postcard that pictured a series of cowboys: *Dudes Descending a Staircase.*

"You know I'm not the least bit resentful," I wrote to him, "about leaving here the most beautiful week in May, just to come out and cook with you," meaning the weather, but he thought, stove, and bought me a bracelet to make up for it.

I knew the plane fare had been a generous gesture, but it made me feel like a concubine, and though I adored the turquoise bracelet, he had to explain why he'd bought it.

I just wanted a tiny picture of the future, not a great request, one week from the summer, a postcard-sized commitment.

I wanted Bogart hugging Bergman, both dressed in white, a still-shot from another moonscape. Arizona was about that dry.

It never stops raining where I come from. Back home I ride the tractor, sing oldies but goodies: *I fought the lawn and the, lawn won. I fought the lawn and the, lawn won.*

The night before leaving I dreamt my eight year old son fell on the summer gravel, and was crying to make your heart break.

I think I was about that age when it started to dawn on me that I was alone in the universe and could depend on no one.

In my dream I was writing with blue chalk: *Something too terrible to remember happened here.*

Now my anxiety slipped off into the desert sunset as he took my hand—We were driving high upon the mesa, color streaking above us—I kept turning around to take it all in, though the opulence seemed to mask some other barrenness.

By sunrise the next morning we were ready to ride. Right off we saw this black and white heifer, chest-deep in mud. We had to gallop for the foreman who wheeled in his truck, roped her, then put his machine into forward—I could see the bubbles as her nose went under.

"Stop!" I yelled, but the cow dogs yipped and the truck kept pulling till she came to herself like a released plug.

The cattle had come down to watch the spectacle, and two bulls started bashing heads. He twirled his horse out of the way without warning. I missed my son already.

I had found him a postcard in the airport. It pictured two

farmers rolling spherical cows: *Just rounding up the cattle.* I missed my house and my own black horse who moved like a machine on water and was as sweet as the summer hay.

Now I rode an old appaloosa with watery eyes. Her canter was akin to the terrain, quite bumpy, and her trot threw me up in the saddle.

Rick didn't like me to gallop, because in his mind it wore wealth from the wallet. "You never want a trotty cow," he said, "because pounds are lost." He never rode for fun, but went out to check the tanks, or cattle or fences. I was used to riding hard and fast.

"I've thought about it," he said to me, "and I just can't see you again till fall. I've got things lined up and I have to stay put."

"So you've already got it decided." I felt like a child, punished for something, I didn't know what. I felt like he'd taken a bucket of earth and thrown it onto my fire.

I would sent him a postcard when I got home, picturing a big ugly fat guy looking at his own reflection—he sees this gorgeous young man: *The Mirror That Lied.*

Still, I always wanted to be a cowboy, and the next morning we saddled up in the semi-dark, jogged our horses down the canyon to the round-up. Like our love, the sunrise was behind us as we rode, and it seemed a shame not to be heading toward it.

I felt lonely yet strangely satisfied. We'd made love a lot since arrival. He had a very dirty mind I'm quite happy to say, and said things which went straight to excite me, like— "Go get an egg from the refrigerator."

He liked to pull up my skirt right there in the kitchen and watch me chop onions. He was built like a bull and liked to get me on the floor. With a close-up of the green bathroom carpet I asked, "Now, what would mother say."

Sitting in the saddle I was still riding in this other dimension, thinking about his verbal courtship, how he told me all

131

the things he was going to do to me. So why did he need so much distance? Why could he only say, I love you, when he thought I was asleep. I kept feeling like an eight year old.

Then I remembered I was holding blue chalk, drawing hopscotch on the back driveway courtyard when my father came out of the house, blood pouring from his forehead — I ran into the kitchen — a broken bottle in her hand — "Why did you *do* that!" I screamed.

"Because I hate him and I wish you were dead," she said to me. "You're just trying to break up my marriage."

I wanted Rick to protect me. He was a big solid man, like an adobe wall. No wonder I couldn't change his mind. I wanted to beat against his chest, not easily moved, and fall asleep with all that weight behind me.

I would write him a postcard when I returned home that pictured three dogs in costume: *Bitch Bitch Bitch,* but my message would be loving and serious: "We're at different places on the same arid mountain. Someday perhaps we'll enjoy the same view."

The slower the cowboys rode the more effective they seemed, though at any moment a horse might dive into a gallop to round up a straggler or escapee. But then the whole group of cattle moved together, as if downstream in the dust of the canyon, bellowing, following, mother and son, following like a moving mob.

"I don't think we can lose 'em," the oldest cowboy grinned, "with the Atlantic on one side and the Pacific on the other."

I remembered now the dream I'd had earlier that morning, my son trying to deliver flowers, but when he got there the party was over and he was bleeding from the throat. An offering that had never met its partner.

I felt a growing resentment over our little *fun* week, and said, "I think I'm going to start charging."

"That's funny," he responded. "I was thinking of charging you."

"What do you mean, a stud fee?" He was the kind of man who could make me beg for it. He liked to talk about inserting things into me, so used to working with animals.

The sun was now before us as we moved the mothers and their calves. Rick's own mother was buried on the ranch, out by Jack's Tank. She was supposedly a very wild lady, who loved to ride fast and had plenty of husbands. I overheard the oldest cowboy saying to Rick, "Doesn't she remind you of someone?" I wondered if that were good or bad.

We had to slowly push the cattle through a gate and then on into the narrowing pasture and corral, where they all huddled as far away as possible.

The eldest cowboy stayed in the saddle and roped a calf by a hind leg, two, if he were lucky, and the little one came skipping backwards across the lot, where two fleshy boys flipped her over and held her, stretched out as the horse backed up, bawling under the boot of America, while I sank to my knees and planted the needle for innoculation. Sometimes there wasn't much meat — I hit bone. One cowboy made a dovetail notch in the left ear, while another clamped a yellow plastic tag on the right. And if it were a bull, they got the balls. "None of this hurts," Rick assured me.

The "rocky mountain oysters" were pulled, pale little sacs with dangling strings, then tossed into the mutts' wide mouths. And then the brand, those facing M's, for Missing Moon, an M with its reflection in water — surely a mirage, for the brand burned through that stinking hair, sizzling to the calf's fresh skin.

I would send him a postcard of a basketball hoop way out in the middle of the desert: "Looking for someone to play with?" But he would have taken the ball and gone home.

Sometimes I wished he didn't have money, this ranch, all fifty-three fucking sections, then he might value me more. But he was thinking of buying an even bigger place, in the red meat center of the universe. It would be more cost effective. He didn't care what the landscape looked like — flat, bare, useless to the eye. The sign on the real estate postcard: *Buy Now Pay Later,* while I predicted mass vegetarianism.

"I can't be in a locked-in relationship with any woman right now. I just have to follow my heart."

"Oh," I said, "I didn't know it was working. How can you even *say* you love me."

"I only said it once," he muttered, as if that didn't count.

"You think you can treat people like cattle?"

I wanted him to achieve the impossible — to love me completely, send the blood back into my father's head.

He decided to sleep on the sofa. I awoke and was frightened by the howl of coyotes and felt his mother's spirit somewhere in the house, not out by Jack's Tank where it was supposed to be.

Rick had likened his mother to an untamed horse, and I wondered if he figured to break me.

I crept through the ranch house in the total dark, begged him back into bed. I would take him in my mouth and give him pleasure.

He always liked for me to do that while he was driving the car. When it got to be too much he'd pull off onto the gravel. I'd be working him hard, then just barely.

"You can't come in my mouth till we're serious," I said, but he caught my head and held me there anyway.

"Now I own you," I swallowed, knowing his response. Something between us was completed.

I thought of him with blood and cow hair on his hands, drinking from that styrofoam coffee, but now he was clean, all shaven and clean, driving me back to the airport.

During the round-up I'd lost a piece of the turquoise from the bracelet he'd given me. It had just dropped out and left a big black hole. "Sort of like your mouth when you take out the tooth," I told him. That didn't stop me from wearing the bracelet, or kissing him either. I actually liked the feeling of putting my tongue where the gap was, but I wasn't going to write him anymore.

In the airport I found a card and was tempted to buy it. It pictured a woman thinking out loud: *Oh my God,* hand raised, she says to herself, *I think I'm becoming the man I wanted to marry!*

STILL SPINNING

The best kisser redefines breathless. One step forward, two steps back. He takes your face in both of his hands. "Guess I haven't been kissed in quite a long time." But it takes two, so you must have been doing your share of kissing him too, and when the kissing stops, the best kissing is when you can't tell, where he left off and you began, his face, yours — it all blurs. He makes motorcycles shine in the dark, makes houses rise — out of the earth. He's good he's bad he's blond in black. What does he want from you. Will he be back? I sure hope so, 'cause life's too slow, without such kissing to make time go. The greatest kisser can fix your machines, overtake your dreams — he gives you honey makes you feel real funny — *Oh baby that's-a what I like!*

OUTSIDE CAREFREE

My sister, Ky, was always the favorite in our family. She had the most beautiful hair, auburn, like my father's, and the most agreeable nature, so much so, I shouldn't have held this unfairness against her.

"My mother couldn't pick me up," I explained to the driver of the limo. "She's up in a hot air balloon at the moment." This was the truth.

There were three balloons floating above the desert presently, multi-colored, huge and lofty. But I was almost relieved to be arriving alone, getting accustomed to the place without the rattle of excitement, all the news cascading down on me in the first three minutes.

Camelback Mountain looked more like a sphinx than a camel, oranges dropping roadside on the bright green grass. The driver paused at the guard gate. We were waved in over the s-l-o-w bump onto the empty paved drive, fashioned to gently roll, a deserted-looking community of creamy white stucco, red-roofed condos. The grounds were well cared for, fruit trees espaliered and hedges trimmed. I noticed the pool, three tennis courts, though I hadn't brought a racket, and had to pay the driver twice as much as my mother had informed me.

No one was at home, but she had left the radio playing, inserted as it was into the kitchen wall. The kitchen itself was wide and sparse, birch wood cabinets without knobs, white counters, an uncooked-in look. The high ceilings of the living room slanted up, and the big glass doors led out to the garden, a fountain trickling water from platter to platter.

This entire yard had been planted four years before. It had been gravel, as the insides had been bare drywall. And now the yard seemed full, palm trees in one corner, bamboo, olive trees and oleander, small cacti and sweet smelling fruit trees. The sweetness made me breathe, delicious, made me realize I *was* in another climate. There was an underground water system that kept the plants in a constant state of no-thirst. But that also meant that the garden had to be hacked back on schedule.

Wandering around inside, I noticed certain antiques I'd known in other homes, the little clay bird I'd made as a child, familiar and unfamiliar paintings. I knew I'd be sleeping in the library on the sofa bed. Ky's room, with the two singles and baby crib was already littered. Ky and her daughter, Pilar, should have arrived around noon.

Just then I heard a car pull up in the driveway. It was the silver-green Volvo with my sister inside it. "Darcy!" she cried, as we rushed toward each other, then almost stopped. "I'm sorry," she said hugging me, "I didn't get you at the airport, but we were seeing Mom off in her balloon. It really scared Pilar. She didn't like seeing Gramma go up."

"It was probably that infernal noise." I kissed Pilar on the top of her head. "I made your baby a new skirt," I said to the real baby, and Pilar, being addressed, jerked her head in the opposite direction.

"There she is," Ky pointed to a balloon that had triangles encircling it, and we heard the momentary roar of its dragon breath. "Anyway Darce," she gave my shoulder a squeeze, "it's nice to have some time alone. You got a perm."

"And you look so thin," I admired her.

"It doesn't even *look* like a perm."

She almost seemed too up, perhaps to make up for the hard words we'd exchanged about this trip. She had been here two times before, and *my* boys hadn't been invited. I was apparently using our mother for this cushy vacation, while she was on some other mission.

"Out of the road," Ky sang to Pilar, with the kind of tone that doesn't mean business, so she didn't move.

"Are these retirement homes, or what?" I asked. Somehow our parents seemed too young for this place.

"Dad even likes it here now," she said. "When he comes."

This was Mom's house. She had bought it after he had gone out and purchased a very mediocre little place in the best suburb of Chicago. He didn't tell her that he'd done it for tax purposes. He simply came home one night and announced, "I bought a house." Arizona was retaliation.

"Do you think we could steam this broccoli?" I wondered, as Ky began tossing pieces in raw. She agreed, and so I steamed some, put it in the freezer to cool. By dinner it was almost frozen. "Can't you just see Mom," I said, as Ky cut tidbits of cornish game hen to add protein to the garden greens, "if she came to visit me, and I didn't pick her up at the airport. Just left a note asking her to go get some food and make dinner."

Ky was still sensitive as to how things would unfold. "I really think Mom is at her best down here. She's so excited for you to see this place."

"It's mighty clean. No wonder mine never appears up to snuff."

"She loves your house. Everything you've done to it."

And everything she'd like to do to it, I thought.

Ky picked up the sweater vest I'd been working on for Mom, a western motif, with horses and cacti, cowboys and hearts. I was using cornflower blue, at her request. "I brought some yarn samples, so you could tell me your favorite colors," I offered.

Ky had been to a color counselor, who had described her as an "Autumn." She had a golden quality to her skin, lovely, long, copper colored hair, wavy and full. She had lost some of that Madonna softness of face, being so slender now. Teal blue was one of her colors, and Mom had bought her a dirndl that color. Mine was an olive green.

"This counselor said some women wear the wrong color on purpose. So they can get sympathy."

I wondered if that were true, or if people just went for the color on the rack. My hair was a dark ash blond, and I was probably an "Early Spring." It made me think of the miserable weather I'd left back home in Connecticut.

Pilar let me button her sweater, but she looked over at Ky all the while, as if to make sure that her mother didn't disappear. "I brought Mom some syrup from the farm," I said. I went to dig out my presents, which included an herbal wreath and a potholder shaped like a fish. The scales were all bright colors, and Pilar wanted to play with it, which was fine with me, but Ky said, "No," and Pilar answered, "*No, you.*"

"Pilar," Ky said firmly, "leave the fishie alone."

She stalked off on her thin little legs, went to the coffee table and threw a magazine on the floor.

"Do you want a spank?" Ky asked nicely, then gave her one. I came in on the whimpering, with the only gift I'd wrapped, for Pilar. A little red wooden horse, with a string attached.

"Oh, it's a Christmas ornament," Ky said. I hadn't realized that, but I guess that's what it had been made for. I held it by the string on my finger, and galloped it along the cold Mexican tiles. I also had a cream colored jersey for Ky, but now I was dying for a swim.

I'd been dreaming of this amniotic moment, and the water was that perfect temperature. An obese older couple was calmly, quietly, swimming laps, getting across, then waiting a bit, before paddling back, while I made waves, goldfish laps. I continued to be amazed at how few people were around, considering that March was such a nasty month back east, and many of these homes, I gathered, were for winter.

142

"Fifty-seven laps equals a mile," the man said. Mom would only be a resident for seven weeks this year. "We've been working our way up to swimming fifteen minutes a day," he said. That didn't seem like long, until I noticed I'd only been at it for five, and felt winded. "Now you must be Mona Marwood's child," he shouted over the burbling swish of the jacuzzi. He was right.

It wasn't long before Mom burst in, certificate in hand, "Here I am!" And I went to give her a hug. "Oh, I wanted to be here to show you the place when you came. But we had the *most* spectacular time!" She was all jumpy. As if I made her nervous. She was tapping the paper, "Here's my certificate." Ky looked interested. "Now Dad and I have *both* gone up."

"Were you afraid?" Ky asked.

"Oh no. It was very peaceful. But you would not believe the size of the houses we went over. Incredible. They looked like hotels, right down Scottsdale Road here. Very tacky, chateaux and Tudor things, these Mediterranean style palatial estates. Monstrous." She was impressed and rejecting the grossness of it all in one breath. "This salad looks divine. Let me just change out of these pants." She wore stretch levis and a cowboy shirt. We were the exact same height, and probably the same weight. She came out of her bedroom in a long house dress, and had to notice my presents now since it was time to set the table. She seemed to like the fish. "This is too pretty to use."

"Mom, look at your vest." Ky ran to get what I'd been working on.

She let her mouth hang open. "*This* is going to be my favorite thing." Was it possible I could please her?

"Do you want some wine, Darce?" Ky asked.

"There's a bottle in the fridge," Mom added. "And these things go in the dishwasher. We did have a little champagne out on the field. It's a tradition."

I went to get my pack of smokes, then followed her out

onto the patio, taking a deep breath, amazingly cooler.

"When the first balloon man landed in this region, the Indians thought he was The Devil, so he broke open a bottle of champagne, and they've been doing it ever since. Darce, are you still smoking? You shouldn't do that."

Before we all faded that evening, Ky came into the guest bathroom in her pink nightgown. I was brushing my teeth with a terrible new toothbrush. My sleep gear consisted of a fresh t-shirt and clean underpants. I started putting away my few toiletries and noticed, "There's no good place to keep this stuff out of Pilar's reach," placing the Ajax up on the counter. "You know you should check the kitchen. Mom never liked to babyproof her house for my kids."

I could see that Ky looked a little disturbed, and had something on her mind. "I just want you to know that I *am* a good mother."

"Are you?" I quipped, but then she looked dejected. "Hey!" I said, "Pilar's great."

"I just thought you'd think it was awful, my giving her that spank. But I think children want to be disciplined."

"I agree." Though I'd never been great on discipline, and personally had no good solution for defiance, possibly because I admired it. Ky didn't seem to lose her temper, and that in itself took a certain amount of discipline.

"You have the first tennis lesson tomorrow morning," she reminded me.

"Oh no. I didn't even bring a racket. I haven't played in years."

"You can borrow mine," Ky offered.

"Just once," I said, kissing her goodnight, as Pilar coughed and turned in her crib.

Next morning, I pulled on my old khaki shorts, laced my grey-looking tennis shoes with zero grip, and went to meet the pro. I liked his spunk. He wasted no time in batting some pretty hard balls my way, and I actually began to enjoy it. He corrected my grip, and after I stopped thinking about "grip" and started to "watch the ball," not "where" it was going, or at him—"Hey, you're a natural," completely dressed in white as he was, very tan, almost handsome, then I felt pretty good, and began to hit some steady shots.

"She'd be terrific if she only played," my mother added, arriving for her tennis lesson early. She always said how great I'd be if I *only* played. The soles of my feet were stinging.

I took care of Pilar, while Ky had her lesson, but in general, I left Ky in charge and didn't feel responsible, just like the weather, which didn't feel demanding, totally relaxed. I did a lot of reading, and let my sister do a lot of dishes. No cup or bowl could be left in the sink. I could see that it was harder on Ky, following Pilar around, making sure she didn't eat the tub soap, but I needed a break, and was taking one.

Mom wanted to show us The Bogata, a shopping mall created to look like an Italian village, with extremely elegant, expensive shops. We had Pilar in the stroller, and Mom insisted that she could keep the baby outside, while we peeked into Pierre Deux and Yves St. Laurent, a generous gesture, I thought, but Ky seemed offended. "Aren't babies fashionable here?"

Mom motioned to a stationery store that sold "dirty" cards she thought were disgusting, while Ky spotted The Face Place. She wore a bit of make-up now, not heavy, just attractive, copper penny lipstick and dark peach blush. She wondered if she could borrow some money.

"Didn't you bring any cash? We just got here," I said, loaning her twenty. We tried on lip liner, and Ky bought some. Pilar wasn't strapped into her stroller, and as she turned to stand, the backrest collapsed, and her head knocked onto the marble floor. We gasped. She screamed, caught her breath, then really screamed, as Ky held her, rocked her and murmured to her, while the girl behind the counter looked at me and tried to suppress a laugh.

Ky urged Mom to go ahead and take me out to lunch. I could see my mother's hesitation, as if she were afraid to be alone with me. "Go ahead!" Ky insisted. "I could use a little time."

"Why don't we all go back and make sandwiches," Mom persisted, but Ky got her way. I wasn't consulted. Why did my mother and Ky have this frankness. Ky could say—"I really dislike that painting in your bedroom. It looks demonic," and Mom would register her response, and later take it down, while I had learned how to be passive, what my sister called, "the polite lie."

"You can never find a place to park around here," she said, "and when you do, the car gets like an oven." But the mid-eighties temperature wasn't oppressive to me. I liked it.

"I bet David loved it here," I said. I knew he had loved the soda pop, the Cheezits and the T.V. set.

"He's the most wonderful child. He just goes along with everything," which meant the adult schedule, late dinners, sleeping in the kitchen. That had upset me, hearing his little voice long distance, saying how he hadn't slept. But David was the kind of boy who just went along. Georgie was more inspired.

"George has a bit of the devil in him," she added. She figured he got that from my husband's side, but he was my baby, and I suddenly missed him terribly. How strong that boy could hug. "George has that look in his eye," she said to finish the picture.

Steele's was a gourmet cafeteria, set in the middle of a country style shop. Mom suggested cold Chinese chicken salad and pasta primavera, but I ordered an artichoke and some carrot *râpé*. Then the awkward moment when I had to get out my wallet before she told the girl at the register that she was paying for mine as well. I hadn't even ordered what she had wanted me to get, so that she could have a taste. We found a table near the window, and I took off my sunglasses, put them on the table. We talked about various members of our family. She was totally estranged from my older brother now, because he had told her to "Shove it," last Christmas. He was on the list of certain people you just didn't bring up. This list included my great-uncle Raymond, because at seventy-nine he had married a thirty-eight year old woman, with a son from a previous marriage.

"That child even tried to electrocute the gardener."

"No."

"He certainly did. The gardener was using electric hedge clippers, and he squirted the man with a hose."

For some reason, when just the two of us were together, it seemed like an opportune time for her to go into one of her raps, which I had to sit through and absorb. When I heard it coming, I tried to hedge it off, but usually she just leapt the hedge and kept going.

"You know Barb Reynolds."

Of course I did. She was the mother of a childhood friend, and I knew she'd been suicidal, that Dad was her broker.

"Did you know that she carried on with Verne Bates for years? Even before they got divorced?" I did know this. I had heard this story at least three times. "Barb's always been emotionally unstable, though she looks just like the perfect little wife. So timid, you know. Well, sweet little Barb arrived at Monnie's house one night with a handgun. Can you believe it? That was after Verne went back to Monnie for a while."

"Can I treat you to some ice cream?" I asked, hoping to change the subject.

"But you know, one night, my husband called me. He was away on a trip." That killed me, when she refered to *my* father, as *her* husband, as if she'd forgotten our relationship. "He said he thought I'd better check on Barb. When I got over to her place, I had to make her let me in, and then she told me how she'd gotten out the sleeping pills, and how she just didn't want to live if he didn't come back to her. She spilled the whole story, business trips, vacations, no one knowing. Can you believe it? But then she said—You'll probably think I'm the worst person in the whole world. But I told her, right then, that the one thing I've learned, is that it's not up to me to judge anyone. But doesn't that just kill you? The most docile-looking women are the ones who're out there trying to steal your husband."

We drove back to the condo, and the guard waved us in. "That guard is the only decent one we have now. The other two don't even know my name."

I had forgotten my glasses.

Ky wanted to have the ice-maker hooked up in the freezer as a present to our mother. Mom said, "Don't bother. I can always buy bags of ice," but Ky convinced her that it might be useful. A plumber would come the next day, while we were at the art museum. The cleaning girl could let him in.

A Mexican girl in her mid-twenties arrived the next morning. She was going to look after Pilar. It didn't look like the place needed cleaning anyway.

On the drive toward the art museum, Ky started in on this rap about milk. "Did you know that there is almost no absorbable calcium in milk?"

"In ordinary store bought milk," I added.

"What other kind of milk is there?" my mother wanted to know.

"Well we drink milk from a local farm," I said. "It's delicious."

"Are you crazy! Unpasteurized milk? Do you want to get typhoid fever? That's just how my brother, Buck Junior, died. Sleeping sickness!"

"It's safe, if the cows are tested. And homogenized milk isn't so great for you either, because the fat particles are spun so fine that they're absorbed more easily into the tissues."

"I can hardly believe *that*. The two of you have gotten in with a bunch of kooks. No decent doctor would agree with you. I can't believe you'd give that to your children."

Instead of letting the whole unfortunate subject drop, Ky went on to deliver her spiel on vitamins. My mother thought vitamin C was for the birds. She had read an article which said just that. "There isn't a professional doctor with any brains who would agree with you, Ky."

"You thought homeopathy was all baloney, until you met that balloon lady," she said.

Where were we to park? She was ruffled. We circled the museum, while she alternated short jerks of the accelerator and brake. I felt too big for the backseat, scrunched. There was a sign for Museum Patron Parking, and Ky pointed, "In there," but Mom insisted that that parking lot was only for the patrons of the museum, meaning, those who supported the museum with large sums of money.

"That's not possible," I chimed in, "for the one big parking lot to be set aside for those few people."

"I guess I know what a patron is."

"It means patrons, like at McDonald's," Ky said. "*Patrons of McDonald's Only*."

"There are two meanings for the word patron," I supplied, trying not to get overly involved in this one.

"Well we're in the wrong place."

"We'll ask at the desk," Ky persisted. They both confused the poor woman behind the desk until Mom looked clearly upset. She walked off alone toward the gift shop after paying for all three of us. Ky realized that she had probably wrecked the rest of the entire week now, but she followed Mom, as I headed towards the Diego Rivera Exhibit.

Ky found me studying a large pastoral scene, which was

neatly diced into wedges of color. Ky told me that Mom had said, "I'll never have you two here at once, ever again. It just doesn't work out." In my mother's mind, I knew, I was to blame.

"We'd better not walk together," Ky said, "or she'll think we're plotting something. I'm sorry," she added. "I don't know why I had to persist in that. I just hate to let her get away with it." Ky always thought it was possible to change her, but I was resigned.

To our amazement, once we all joined up again, Mom was back in a decent mood. She had let it pass. She had gathered her equilibrium and decided—I'm not going to let this bother me—we are going to get along. She was even up for stopping at Loehman's on the way back.

Ky still had no cash, but she assumed she'd be able to use her credit card. I wanted to find one nice cotton jersey, and did, periwinkle blue and cerise red.

Ky had a stack of things, and a lot of it looked good on her. She decided against the skirt, but wanted the dress, two shirts and pants, even though the dress wasn't exactly one of her colors.

When she came back into the dressing room she announced, "They don't accept credit cards." Now what would she do.

"I can get yours," my mother said to her. "You can always pay me back."

I headed for the counter with my jersey, and bought it, twelve bucks.

That evening we were going to go get Mexican food, because Ky liked it, but Dad didn't, and he was arriving the next day. We were all going to wear our dirndls. Mom had one too, without the scooped neckline, which only Ky filled out. Even Pilar had a baby blue dirndl. We must have looked like we walked into the wrong flavor of restaurant, ordering a pitcher of margaritas. A piñon fire was burning out on the patio, smelling of mountain nuts, sweet sage and desert night-time, while the evening sky was clear with brilliant points of light. The dark ridge of the mountains stood out and the saguaro cactus looked postcard perfect. Shapes seemed more pure and visible on the desert. Both of them wiped the salt off of their glasses, but that was my favorite part.

The plumber had come to connect the ice-maker in the freezer, but there still appeared to be no water in the trays. Mom was furious. Ky called the plumber back, and he said that the machine must not be working.

"This is a brand new refrigerator," my mother spoke over their conversation. "Any plumber in the world knows how to connect these things. Tell him you're going to cancel the payment."

Ky's voice was gentle, sincere, and kind on the phone, while our mother kept up her own argument, "You have to stand over these people, make sure they do their jobs."

I was getting anxious to see some of the real desert. I'd begun to feel the excess of opulence in this suburb, where Mercedes were more common than pick-up trucks.

"Do you think we could go riding, out at Carefree?" I asked.

"You're riding Sunday, near Castle Hot Springs," she answered, with a look that said— Nothing is ever enough for you.

"I'd love to see Carefree though." An hour out of Phoenix. To my amazement, she picked up the phone and dialed The Carefree Inn, made reservations for Saturday morning.

Dad had arrived that night, looking totally worn out. He took off his suit and put on some tennis shorts, lay down on their king-sized bed and went immediately to sleep. Chicago had been freezing. Hard to conjure winter now. Plus there had been a minor tragedy at the airport. Mom had been carrying Dad's cowboy hat, and she'd put it on the roof to the Volvo and driven off.

I sat on the sofa with my knitting, and threw a big ball of yellow yarn for Pilar, who ran gleefully to collect it, bringing it right back to me, so that I'd throw it again.

"Is that the yarn for my sweater?" Mom wanted to know. "It's going to get dirty rolling around on the floor."

"Nothing could get dirty on this floor," I assured her, throwing it again. I had finished the back and almost one side of the front.

"Well please don't eat that in the living room."

She went to open two cans of chilled Campbell's soup, beef bouillon, which we were to have for dinner. The gelatinous globs looked sickening to me, and I decided to cook some frozen lima beans.

"You can't use those," she said.

"Why not?"

"Because it's my house, Darcy, that's why."

In the past, Mom would have felt left out, cheated, and she would have been angry and made us all feel guilty about leaving her behind, but now after a good night's sleep, she was actually in a pleasant mood, and up for a morning with Pilar.

Ky lingered over Pilar, "Bye sweetheart, bye-bye. Will you be a good girl? Take care of Gramma."

I hopped in the front seat, leaning forward to let Ky in the back.

"You can have the front coming back," Dad said to be fair.

"I don't mind the backseat," she said.

Dad seemed dreamy as usual. He always looked like he needed another cup of coffee. When you spoke to him, it was as if you were jarring him out of some deep and distant thought.

"Where'd you get David's cowboy belt?" I asked.

"How is my Dave?" he answered.

"You know the one with his name engraved on the back?" David, my son, was his namesake. Both of my parents seemed to cater more to Dave, perhaps because he was older and could do more things, or because he looked like a Marwood.

"Does Georgie still have that white blond hair?" Ky asked.

"You had the exact same hair," my father commented, as if he were shaking off hibernation. "The most lovely, light blond hair," he mused, and I felt almost hopeful. "But the most *beautiful* hair in the family," he went on, and my heart sank, even though I was prepared for this anecdote, heard so often throughout my childhood, "was Ky's, those gorgeous red brown curls. Just like mine," he teased.

I looked back at Ky, who was looking out the window. I wondered if she liked this story, or if it embarrassed her. She probably thought I was way above it.

"I hope Mom didn't mind staying home," Ky said, distantly, as if she were picturing Pilar.

"We can make it up to her," Dad put in, "by all playing tennis this afternoon." Mom was a different person when she got her tennis. That was certainly true.

It was a bright, warm morning, and the desert terrain was clear for miles. One could see the spine of the continuing range, the long stretches, and then the fancy houses perched amongst the boulders.

The Carefree Corral was filled with many unspectacular horses, and the air, with a light dust. Walking up to the shanty, a blond mother cowgirl got our names. Her daughter, about twelve, came out of the adjoining trailer. I asked her if she got to ride much, but she said, "Naw, mostly school."

I bent to tie my silly looking shoes. I wasn't exactly dressed appropriately, in my yellow overalls, while Ky looked authentic, in her blue jeans with real Western boots, a levi jacket, her auburn hair pulled back in a ponytail.

"Experienced, or inexperienced," the mother from inside the little shack wanted to know. Her daughter slouched at the door.

"We're experts," I said, knowing you had to boast in order not to get a total plug.

"They're experts," the girl repeated for her mother with a grin.

"We've been riding since we were two," I added.

"Riding since they were two," she repeated for her mother, who then came out and approached me and my sister.

"Which one of you is the better rider?" she asked.

I waited a second, then said, "I am," and could see my sister flinch, even though it was the truth and she knew it.

"Well, I'll take the one with the boots for Maytag," she said, and my sister skipped eagerly to her horse, a chestnut, as if she'd won some contest without even having to pipe up.

The slightly punier Prince suited me fine, and Dad got a horse named Flake, short for Snowflake. We could ride by ourselves, without a guide, so they had believed us. Dad led the way out of the ranch on his less than snow white steed, taking a narrow hill trail. The land was extremely dry and bare, lots of rocks, and the cactus snagged my pants. I felt exposed without the protective leather of boots, and was afraid of seeing a rattler. They were appearing this time of year, and I pictured old Prince rearing, my foot getting caught in the stirrup, dragged down this rocky terrain. So I concentrated on keeping my heels down, reins relaxed, as Prince followed. Ky moved her horse off to the left, picking a slightly steeper ascent, but I followed my father as we climbed, until we finally crossed a paved road and entered an abandoned development, no houses yet, just windy lots. Black plastic flapped and our horses balked, then skittered backward. The view from up here was fantastic, though the heat glazed our vision.

We rode down a dry stream bed, cantering our horses along through the sand, safer than those rocky trails, though tiring for the horses. But then the river bed stopped, dead end, and Ky spotted a common cow skull. She wanted to get off and pick it up. "Somebody might want it."

"Who, Georgia O'Keeffe?" I said.

"Where would you put it," my father asked, disconcerted.

Oh well, what did it matter. She turned her ebullience back to a good return run. Dad's horse didn't seem to want to move faster than a trot, and I kept mine at a gentle lope.

Then we spotted what looked like a covered wagon, as if we'd ridden right onto a stage set. Riding closer, we smelled breakfast smells, then saw that it was a chuck wagon, set up for a breakfast ride. A big group was coming in soon, and he gave each of us a cup of orange juice. He had the biggest silver belt buckle I'd ever seen, with a bucking bronco raised in gold on top of the engraved silver.

My father sniffed the air for a cup of black coffee, but it wasn't ready yet. "If you go on down this creek," the cowboy pointed, "you'll find Clown Rock, and you go on through that gulch, and then you'll find a whole mess of trails."

We headed that way, politely, but just beyond the rock stood a big black bull. When he stood up his balls hung down, and he seemed to sink slightly in the sand. We turned our horses, but he didn't move, more cautious than Midwestern cows, who always crowded up very curious. Here they probably figured we were aiming to round them up, brand them, send them off to Chicago for the purple stamp.

We took a very steep hillside trail, and Ky's horse almost slipped. I wondered if we shouldn't get off, lead the horses. "This is treacherous." We were well off the beaten track, but we all managed to stay in the saddle. Long whip-like cacti had stunted blossoms on each end. Between two barrel cacti, Dad spotted a lizard, which lay breathless on a rock. Dad would love to see a snake, I knew, but I wanted to see the little town of Carefree. Even my brother and sister-in-law had been impressed with Carefree, mother had said, "And you know how nothing impresses them."

We crossed back over the same paved road, and passed

a mother and her son, both on horseback. It made me miss my boys, how I'd love to be riding with both of them. The ranch was in sight now, and Ky spotted something long and dark, that she thought was a dead snake. But then she recognized it as a piece of leather. Dad and I both rode by, kept going down the trail for home. She got off her horse to pick up the piece of bridle, thinking that the ranch could use it.

Down below, I slid out of the saddle, felt the relaxed relief of being back, and handed over the horse to a cowboy, who suddenly jerked to look, and yelled out, "Horse in without rider!" I turned and saw Maytag galloping down the slope. I wasn't surprised, thought he'd broken away from Ky, when she'd gotten off, but the cowboy was already on his Arabian, dashing up the hill, another quick to follow. Dad and I stood there. I figured she'd come trotting down on her own two legs in a moment. But then we heard a loud wail of a moan, that didn't sound natural, maybe a joke, but Dad said, "I'd better go up," and I simply stood there, just looking in that direction, unable to see anything but the dusty chapparal, sure that she was just kidding, but then it struck me—Maybe something *was* wrong. Why was I standing there? To make up for the lack of impulse, I raced up the slope, tripping on rocks, and saw her there on the trail, lying on her back, knees up, the three men bent over her. "My God," I said, as her face contorted. She motioned to the sharp low rock. No one was talking. She tried to speak, "He bucked me, when I— I was—" she jerked from the pain. "I can't, breathe," she whispered, trying to turn herself onto her side.

"Don't move," I insisted.

"Bit of leather," she waved, "over there." But the cowboys didn't want it. Her forehead was tense, compressed. "My rib. My . . ." She could barely speak.

"I'll call an ambulance," I told my father. He was mute with worry, immobilized, kneeling over her.

New dude ranch riders were standing around down below,

looking worried, and the blond mother manager looked peeved as she let me use the phone. The sign over the shanty read: *Not responsible for Accidents of Any Kind.* I ran back up the hill. "They're coming babe," I put my hand on her forehead. "Try to relax."

"Hurts so bad," she winced. We heard the siren. "They'll be here in no time now. You're going to be much much better. I'll run down," I told Dad, but he followed me this time. I felt like crying. Poor baby sister, foolhardy kid.

As we stumbled back into the corral, we saw a chartreuse fire truck. Why had they sent that? No stretcher, no place to ride, but they had oxygen and a big black bag. My father pointed the way up, but said he would wait for the ambulance. "At least we were close to home," I offered.

"We could have brought in a chopper," one said. Routine for them. Ky was trying not to writhe, mouth open, wanting more air. They got the oxygen tubes up her nostrils, turned it on. She could get air now without trying so hard. They took her blood pressure, while the Arabian yanked at its thick rope, tied to a bush. "Nice horse," I mentioned to the cowboy, who was smoking a cigarette. I didn't ask for one. The emergency man lifted Ky's shirt up, and you could see her flesh colored bra, a long red hook mark across her ribs. The rock had been small, but a sharp one. She'd taken a jagged bite inside. The mother and son were riding back down the trail now, and I ran to head them off, then heard the ambulance coming.

Walking back up, Dad looked grey with concern. The driver had a stretcher, and when they lifted her up to strap her in, she made hurt little animal sounds, sharp small cries. I tried to hold her hand as we descended, but they told me not to touch the stretcher. "She's in terrible pain," I said. "Can't you give her something?"

"Not till she's been checked out. It might mask the symptoms." But the clinic was only minutes away, and that at least seemed lucky.

Dad indicated that I should ride up front in the ambulance. He would follow. They strapped my seat belt for me, as if I were a child. The oxygen in the ambulance didn't want to work at first, so the man in back thumped the container with his boot, got it going. He continued to take her blood pressure. The dirt road was bumpy, good to finally reach a paved road. But after another mile of smooth cruising, the man in back said, "OK, Bob, let's make it party time."

"Will do," the driver answered, as he flicked on a switch near his visor, and the siren started up, and he put on speed, as we buzzed over a cattle guard, and I said, "What's wrong?"

He answered calmly, "Her blood pressure's dropping." I looked out the window, started to cry. I could see Dad's silvergreen Volvo in pace with us, thought of Mom at home with Pilar, knowing nothing about this. It sounded so quiet in the backseat. The siren was absolute and loud. I imagined some spirit made out of desert brightness, hovering close to our speeding vehicle. We squealed into the parking lot. The entire staff of the tiny clinic was standing outside, waiting with a gurney. A doctor had been called. Ky looked pale as they pulled her out, limp. Some technician got scissors, and they cut off the cream-colored turtleneck I'd given her.

"So much for that shirt," I whispered to her.

"Don't make me laugh," she tried to smile, but then wakened to the pain. Inside, I was beside her, holding her hand firmly, as if I could give her something.

"We're going to do x-rays now," the man said to me. "Can you stand over there?"

"Will you call Mom," she asked me. "I'd like her to pray."

I let Dad call. He was concerned in tone, quietly firm. Pilar was already napping. "Don't forget to tell Mom to pray," I reminded him, and the nurse smiled over at me, "I don't think he has to tell her." I felt like an efficient jerk.

Four badly broken ribs, displaced. They couldn't tell about the lung. She'd have to be transferred to Phoenix. She was being given Demerol for the pain, and was beginning to relax, to sleep. Dad called Mom again, delivered this news, while I unpeeled the sweetest, juiciest grapefruit I'd ever eaten. Even the peel came off without any reluctance. Dad was too distracted to try some. He told me to ride in the ambulance again, though I would have preferred riding with him. He probably didn't feel like talking. Ky was almost out now on the medication, and the driver was silent, so I knit. I was working on the front band where the buttons would be sewn.

We were almost to the city limits, when I asked if there were ever any rodeos in town.

"Best rodeo in the world, going on right now," the driver answered. "Right in the downtown arena." Seemed odd to me, having a rodeo inside a building. "Jerry works emergency there. Hey, Jerry," he said, and the man moved forward so that he could talk.

"Yeah, those cowboys get pretty broken up," Jerry added. "Last night one got trampled." It didn't seem right to talk about this with Ky lying there in the back.

"Were you worried," I asked Mom, "when Dad called?"

"Not so much the first time." She now appeared very nervous, gathering her sweater, purse, hat, getting ready to go.

"It's a jagged break," Dad said, sounding serious. His voice always dropped when he was upset.

"Well how are they going to get them back together?" Mom complained, her voice increasing. "She didn't puncture a lung, did she?"

"I don't think they can tell yet."

I had been worrying about her lung, because she'd had such trouble breathing, but that might have been from the pain.

Mom wondered if we should cancel our reservations at Mancuso's for that evening. "Oh!" she said, disgusted. "If only we'd taken a picture of us all in our dirndls!" Now it would be too late. "Well I guess if Ky's in the hospital, and we have a babysitter anyway, we might as well go."

I was in charge of Pilar now. I took her tiny hand, and she looked up at me. Mother had set up a playpen, where she had dumped all the toys. Pilar didn't want to go near it. I got out the salad spinner, put a cork inside and showed her how to give it a whirl.

"Where's Lucy?" I asked about her doll, and Pilar looked concerned, hunting around.

"Oh here she is," I called, finding the doll wedged between two cushions of the sofa. "Looks like she's ready for supper."

"Go," Pilar announced, heading for the kitchen.

I began the meal by introducing alfalfa sprouts. Pilar liked pulling them out of the plastic carton, like easy grass, but the texture on her lips was tickly. She made a funny face, sticking out her chin, surprise, delight, disgust, curiosity, wanting to pull out some more just for fun. She had big dark eyes. "China doll," my mother called her. "She looks just like a china doll. But it'll be nice when she gets more hair, some bangs to cover that great big forehead."

"I like her forehead the way it is," Ky had responded, unabashed.

Pilar wanted to feed herself the soup, though mother had thought we shouldn't let her, because she made too much of a mess.

"They have to make a mess, if they're going to learn," was my opinion, but she obviously needed a bath after dinner.

It was wonderful, holding that bare little body, helping to splash her all clean. She loved the water, but didn't fuss when I said it was time to get out. Patting her dry, I then wrapped her up tight, swung her into my arms like a little papoose, so much lighter than my big boys. It brought back sensations, but she was something different. My boys had always struggled to get down, while she was alert and responsive, eye to eye. I had always wanted a daughter.

Mancuso's had a deceptively small entrance. Once inside, the place opened up into a massive space, with mirrors on the back wall, doubling the illusion, two stories up to the ceiling. Long sculptural chandeliers dangled down. There were in timatc booths, and ours was in the middle of the room. "I think in a fancy place like this, it's not right to have booths," my mother said. "Everybody wants to see everybody else."

"But it does make it quieter," I noticed. "So we can talk."

We decided against hors d'oeuvres, since we'd all been overeating. The dinner came with salad, *soupe aux champignons*, and a sorbet between courses. Mom and I both ordered *fettuccine Alfredo*, which was delicate and rich, freshly made pasta. Dad was ready to fall asleep. He spoke only when spoken to. I think he had learned how to rise above and block out most of what we women said, but I was surprised that they didn't speak about Ky with much concern now.

"We might as well go to Castle Hot Springs tomorrow, as planned," Mom said. "With Ky in the hospital, there's nothing much we can do." I was shocked by this attitude, but was also ready to go along. Dad and I were to ride with Betty Benson. The Bensons had no telephone at their retreat. The luncheon and ride had been prearranged in Chicago. "We don't leave until ten, but it's a two hour drive." We shared a white chocolate mousse for dessert. I had never in my life had dinner with just the two of them before. I doubted if they were aware of that.

"Be back by quarter of ten," mother told me. "I still have to get gas and pick up some grapes for this salad." She had agreed to make lunch, chicken salad, and the Bensons would provide the dessert and the drinks. I was anxious to see Ky, and sped over the guard bump. Dad was taking care of Pilar.

Ky seemed glad to see me, with the grapefruit she'd

requested. I helped position her bed, and got the phone within easier reach. "Have you talked to Jeffrey?"

"Last night," she barely smiled. "I told him not to come."

"I heard Dad talking to him last night too. Dad told him to fly out here, that he'd pay for it."

"I guess he decided not to."

"But you're going to need help with Pilar, once I go. Maybe Mom will find a babysitter, or I could take Pilar back with me. The boys would love to have her visit. You know it's going to be hard lifting her, travelling and everything."

"That's sweet of you, but I don't think I could stand having her that far away."

"You know I got her to eat some vegetables last night."

"You did?"

"And I got her to sleep before the babysitter came."

"Oh thank you," she said, looking immensely tired.

"Mom took her into their bed this morning, early, but I'm afraid there's a little tension there. Pilar sort of pushes her away."

"I know," Ky said. "I don't know what to do about that. Do you think Mom's mad that I ruined the vacation?" I didn't think so. "Dad thinks I was a fool, getting off like that."

"Hindsight's always 20/20. But a dude ranch horse shouldn't buck like that. Do you think they gave you the better horse?"

"Well, you didn't exactly *look* like any expert." She tried not to laugh. "I just feel terrible, that you were supposed to have a break, and now you're taking care of Pilar."

"I love it," I said. "I was just letting you take care of her, but I was missing out."

"Do you think you could bring her here tomorrow?"

A candy striper pulled up to the room. Ky wanted a Mounds bar, and some stationery, but didn't have money, so I got it for her.

"It's funny," she went on, "but now I'm actually getting

the rest I needed. I make so little time for that."

"You had me pretty worried yesterday, when that guy said, Party Time."

She nodded. "But you know, I said to myself, I'm really not afraid to die. It would be perfectly all right, if it weren't for Pilar."

"Are you happy?" I asked. "I mean, with Jeffrey?"

She paused, and thought about that, but didn't have a ready answer.

"I called Dan yesterday," I said. "We literally talked for about two minutes before he had some excuse to get off. He wouldn't do that to any other person on earth, not even a stranger."

"At least you're not living with a stranger," Ky added.

"I told you to be back by 9:30," Mom said, wheeling around, grabbing her pocketbook.

"I thought you said ten."

"You can put on my levis, they're on the bed. And change shirts." She left for the grocery store. I guess I didn't look right. The levis were the stretch ones, rather stiff and scratchy, not my style, but at least they fit me. I went ahead and put on a white oxford cloth shirt, my Foreign Legion hat, instead of the cowboy hat she'd arranged for me to wear. It was too small, and perched on top of my head.

When she got back, she loaded up the ice chest. "Why aren't you wearing the cowboy hat," she wanted to know. "I put it out for you."

I strapped Pilar in her car seat, got in back myself. I was already scrunched, but then Mom jammed her front seat back even further. "I have a bad knee, Darcy."

I picked up my knitting, trying to convert hostility into rows. It seemed to take a long time getting out of town, even though Scottsdale was on the outskirts. Pilar responded to the finger games I played, and then I sang her songs until she fell asleep.

"She won't take an afternoon nap now," my mother commented.

Finally, we turned off onto a dirt road. Dad said we had to take it for another fourteen miles. How could anyone build so far away from everything.

"You know Betty would move in an instant," Mom said. "This is really no man's land. They don't even have a phone out here."

"I think they chose not to have a phone," Dad said.

"Marjorie Perlhoff had a helicopter bring her and a party out here. I won't even guess what that cost, but I guess Marjorie has money to throw away."

We drove and dipped and bumped on, even splashed through a little creek, squeezed through tiny canyon passes, a bright green cottonwood by the water, shock of color against the desert dryness, joggling onward. I held Pilar's head from bouncing too much. I had wanted to say something more to my sister—You know I would take good care of her.

Finally Pilar wakened, started to squirm and fuss. She was hot and I let her out of her car seat, while my mother handed her a cookie, told her to "Shh, shh," like a broom sweeping a mess away. The cookie was a good distraction, but a bad idea. When would we ever get there. Mom pointed out Hell's Gate, so we were getting closer. We were all thirsty and hot and hungry by the time Mom spotted some familiar corral, where we took a right, went another mile up their driveway to this amazing house perched on the top of a mountainous rock. Getting out, the view became a 360 degree panorama, as if they owned their own county, miles and miles in every direction, range upon range, layers and more distant layers of subtle color, with no other house in sight, just one red winged hawk circling above in the silent desert air. The light was powerful. "Isn't this the most beautiful place you've ever seen?"

My mother's mood was now exalted, as they kissed and exchanged their greetings, familiar friends from Chicago with this Arizona second-home interest in common.

The house was western magnificent, huge Navaho rugs on the living room floor with its high pitched ceiling, wooden fan, a large Charles Russell painting over the massive fireplace. The eight foot windows offered an endless look out. "We got these windows from the Phoenix Country Club," Mr. Benson said, showing us around.

"You mean you salvaged them from there?" I asked.

"Ho, ho, that's a good one!"

"He means, we copied them," Betty explained, leading us back onto the patio, where we'd have our lunch on a redwood picnic table. She opened a bottle of Chardonnay.

I wondered if they minded being disturbed up here in their hideaway. She said how eager she was to have riding companions, how much she loved it here, and that they had plenty of visitors to keep them company, all of which was fine.

"Betty," he boomed, "tell them about last Sunday." There was a lasso hanging by the door, two pairs of leather chaps.

"I have this mustang, you'll see him later," she began. "He's quite spirited, and I was just riding along, when I took off my hat, and it scared him. The next thing I knew I was on the ground."

"Completely ruined her good jacket," he said, as if that were a great joke. The ripped suede jacket was also hanging on the hook by the door. "But one little aspirin took care of her."

I found myself liking Betty. I liked her manner, her simple worn-in clothes. I liked the fact that she rode horses, though she was over sixty, liked the way she talked about her children. Some of them I knew. I even liked the fact that she loved this no-man's land. She hadn't been hauled off here against her will, for they seemed as happy as two mice in a great big boot.

As we walked down to the corral, it was windy, a hollow

wind, like the sound of a bottle blowing. She pointed out the hideout where Indians used to go when white men came. She told me that she had even been on some round-ups with the cowboys who lived on the closest ranch. I asked her if I could ride the all-white horse. His coat was as soft as a bunny.

When we returned to Scottsdale, it was almost five o'clock. Dad called the hospital, and found out that Ky's lung had been punctured. They were going to have to perform an operation on the following day. It meant pushing a tube into her lung to drain it. Dad didn't wait for Mom to get ready. He went over immediately. When he returned, he said that Ky wanted to see Pilar in the morning. There were no rules against children in the hospital anymore.

Mom was having an early tennis lesson that morning, so Dad dropped me off with the baby. I had suggested that it might be easier if we didn't all go together.

"Sweetheart!" Ky crooned, opening her one arm. The other arm stayed close to her body. "Put her on this side," she instructed me, and then groaned as Pilar climbed up onto her. "You know I don't think she recognized me at first. Forgotten your Mama?" But they hugged, hard, kissed and hugged again. "My sweetest baby darling!" I had to help and try to keep Pilar back down, on the one side, but now my touch seemed to sting her. She wanted Mama with all her might. "Mama has a hurt, a bad hurt," Ky pointed to her ribs. "You stay right there." But Pilar wanted to squirm all over her mother, and when I tried to pick her up, she screamed. Then a nurse came in, and said that Ky had to be rolled down to x-ray again, but the baby could ride along. It would just be a minute.

"My breathing is still real bad, but this operation is supposed to be routine. They even do it right in my own bed."

The nurse was ready now, and she wheeled Ky out. Pilar

settled down for the ride, and I kept my hand on the small of her back.

Mom and Dad appeared shortly, down in x-ray, while we were waiting for Ky's turn out in the hall. We chatted there for a moment. Mom wanted to take me shopping that afternoon, since this was my last day. I would have been willing to stay on, help take care of Pilar, if asked, or if they needed me. Mom had not found a babysitter, and she was getting anxious about that. She was about to call Mercy in Chicago, see if she could fly out. Mercy helped her clean, also helped with the grandchildren when they came to visit.

Dad appeared with a stuffed horse, gave it to Pilar. Buying stuffed animals was an impulse he couldn't resist. But now it was time to drag Pilar away. Dad picked her up and she began to wail, but he kept walking away with her, so then Ky started to cry as well, "I don't want him to take her away like that."

"Don't be silly," mother said. "Any baby's going to cry. You know she's going to stop as soon as she's around that corner."

I whipped up our lunch, made a green salad, a dressing, then put the leftover chicken salad in the middle with a few green grapes on top. Pilar wanted grapes, reaching, grunting. "You have to eat some peas first," I insisted, and helped her, then gave her one grape. "Eat some more, and I'll give you a bunch." She was even getting fussy with me now. I toasted some English muffins, put butter on the table. Dad began eating right away. Mother was still changing. "Would you like some coffee or a beer?" I asked him. He was reading the paper as he ate.

"Beer," he smiled up at me, "and *then* coffee."

"I thought we were having chicken sandwiches!" Mom said. Seeing the luncheon I'd served up made her angry.

"Well stuff some into a sandwich if you want to—that shouldn't be too hard." I sat down, and started to eat, though the sudden emotion cancelled my appetite. She didn't bother to change my layout, and was quick to change her mood. Maybe it was better when I did react.

Actually, it was remarkable, how she persisted in trying to show me a good time. Dad had agreed to babysit Pilar while we went shopping for an hour. She was looking for an apricot shirt that would go with a plaid skirt she'd brought along, but the spring colors were all peach, a shade off.

I spotted a plain white cotton dress, like a long sweatshirt, with big pockets, long sleeves and a belt. "Do you like this?" I asked her.

"It's all right," she said. I realized she wasn't interested in looking for me.

I decided to try the dress on anyway. She quickly found something to try on too. I liked the way the white gave me more color. Tomorrow I'd be back to deep drifts. This dress would hang in my closet for months. I tried tightening the belt buckle that came with it, an odd slip-and-grip kind of attachment, and as I pushed it, a sliver of metal buried itself into my index finger and began to bleed. The dot of blood expanded as I held out my hand, away from the white material. The salesgirl rushed to get me a kleenex and a bandaid. Mom offered to buy the dress.

Dad was ready to go when we got home. It had taken us longer than we thought. But just after he pulled out, a nurse called from the hospital and said that Ky didn't want anyone visiting for a couple of hours. She was too tired from the operation. I informed the nurse that the patient's father might arrive at any time.

He actually did arrive to hear my sister screaming. He was not allowed to go into her room. They had given her over twenty shots of novocaine to numb her chest area, but she didn't realize what they were giving her. She was insensitive to novocaine. They were performing the entire operation with her fully awake, feeling everything.

Dad stood up, walked down the hallway.

After it was over, he went in and held her hand. The doctor was in a complete sweat. She cried when she knew that Dad had heard her.

When he returned home, he looked drained, elsewhere. Mom was in the bedroom, talking to Ky on the phone, cursing the damn doctors, how you couldn't trust anybody in a hospital you didn't know, how they should have called somebody. Why didn't they give her gas? Why did they use novocaine? Why didn't anybody know anything! Mom came out of the bedroom wiping her eyes. "She could feeling them pushing that tube right into her," Mom cried, "through her ribs, and muscles and everything."

"She wants Darcy to come over tonight," Dad said. "Ky's going to have to stay in for quite a while. They're worried about pneumonia."

"Maybe I shouldn't go home," I offered, hoping that Pilar didn't understand all this.

"Well I reached Mercy today, and she's going to fly down for a week." My mother was pleased.

"What if Ky has to stay in for more than a week?" I mentioned.

"I'm sure we can figure it out," she said, indicating she wasn't an idiot. "Mercy can sleep in your bed."

I had on the new white dress Mom had bought me, and it looked good, cinched with the navy belt. My hair was clean and bouncy-looking. I'd put on a bit of Ky's blush-on, her copper penny lipstick. I felt urgent about getting to the hospital now.

Ky lay back on her bed looking shattered, like a victim of violence, extreme, the bloody nightgown still displaying her wound, the color sucked out of her skin. This was the second layer of physical shock she had suffered, and it had taken the light right out of her. I kissed her immobile cheek.

"It was like torture," her voice was hushed, "like the Civil War. I felt the entire thing. Like someone taking out a bullet with a knife."

"Oh babe," I groaned.

"I didn't realize they were using novocaine. It never works at the dentist."

"No one asked you?"

"I don't think so."

"You know, when I had that spinal, with David, they gave me a shot, and waited a bit, but as soon as they went in, I felt the whole works, as if they were pulling my insides out."

"Maybe it's hereditary," she said.

I felt badly, having brought the reference back to myself, to qualify, not to nullify, but it seemed to lessen the impact of what she'd just been through. I reassured her about Pilar, how she had been a perfect baby, how Ky had done a great job with her. "Mercy's coming down for a week."

"Oh good," Ky said.

"I'd stay if you needed me."

"You have to get back to your boys."

"She might act terrible, when you move back to Mom's. They always make you pay, no matter how good they've been with the babysitter."

"You've been much more than a babysitter."

"I think Jeffrey should come out here. You can't fly home alone." I had thought about calling him myself, letting him know what Ky had been through, how serious it looked. I felt badly that we'd been out shopping right when she was having that operation.

"Great dress," Ky said, and I did a spin.

"Mom bought it. So I guess I can forgive you about Loehman's."

"Don't be so dumb." She smiled a small smile.

"Well you can be a brat you know." I hugged her, and we both started to cry, then laughed. I could tell that she was exhausted, but I wanted to clear the board. "I even felt hurt," I admitted, "when Dad brought up that old thing about your hair. The most beautiful hair bit. Even if it is true."

"Well some of us are better riders."

"Right," I laughed. Enough said.

"But you know what's odd? I always thought that I was jealous because of Dad, but it isn't that, it's Mom, that the two of you can talk, that you can say what you mean. I guess I've always been trying to get her to love me."

"And she does," Ky answered, quietly. "She just doesn't know how."

Maybe Ky was right, but that didn't make it any easier.

Ky requested a backrub. "Dad wouldn't do it," she complained. "He was afraid of knocking the tube." The tube went right into her chest, and back out, draining. A machine by the bed made a watery, bubbly sound. Ky smelled like formaldyhyde. "My breathing is already better. If you can slide your hand down in, behind." I eased my hand in, behind the dead weight of her body, which she couldn't lift, and found the place where the knot of tension had lodged, like a hard rock, just beside her wingbone.

"You probably had a muscle spasm from all that pain." I pushed hard against the tightened knot of muscle. She smelled like sour salad dressing. I rubbed and rubbed harder, and she liked it — I rubbed until my hands were almost cramping, then rested a while, poured her some soda on ice. "I don't want to tire you out," I said to her, still wanting to visit, since this was my last night.

"I don't love my husband," she said then. "I don't know what I'm going to do."

She asked me to lower her bed, and I did, about four inches. She looked so distant, so tired. "I really miss Pilar."

171

I'd see my boys tomorrow. I hadn't bought David a present yet. Maybe I could find him something at the airport, a lasso, or some cactus candy. Presents were hard at his age. David was Ky's godson, and they had a nice relationship.

"I had this uncomfortable scene with David before I left," I told her. "We were looking for a ski sweater, for his birthday, and we found one we both liked, a real pretty shade of blue with white racing stripes, on sale, and he wanted it, until he spotted this other one, which was grey and olive and black. I said I'd get him the baby blue one, but he only wanted the drab one then. He even said that he'd have that one, or neither."

"So what did you do?"

"I didn't get him either one, and felt horrible."

"Couldn't you go back and get the ugly one?" she asked.

"I guess so."

"Would you give it to him for me? I'll pay you back, I promise," she smiled. Then she asked me to turn off the light.

Pilar threw me a kiss, and another kiss, another, as Dad and I left that morning. We drove off, sitting quietly for a while.

"Do you think Ky's lung is serious?" I asked him.

"I don't think it's going to be bad now." He slapped my knee a couple of times, and asked, "Did you have a good vacation?" And then he was off, dreaming again, I could tell.

I was back in the same winter clothes I'd worn on arriving, and when we pulled up at Sky Harbor, I told him not to wait. I could check the bags right through, right there on the sidewalk.

I gave him a hug goodbye, taking one last look at the clear blue sky and desert landscape before entering the building's sliding glass doors that parted as I approached them.

THE RIGHT SKATES

The hand of the famous artist was warm when I met him, but then it was also freezing cold outside. I had written him a fan letter about his recent exhibition, and sent along a book of my own. I think he must have liked the photo on the dust jacket, because he called me immediately, all fired up, and invited me down to the city.

I didn't dare say — I don't really look like that, but suggested we meet at this gallery — the sculptor was a woman friend of mine, and the show was delightful — long, sculpted sticks that had been painted and bent into an airborne dimension.

I felt lively yet relaxed walking around the space, reading the names of the pieces.

"The titles don't matter," the famous artist said. He was almost twenty years older, lanky, severe. "I like this work," he added.

The sculpture reminded me of the arrows of Artemis, of giant ice-fishing hooks. I was pleased he could appreciate the work of a woman, a sure sign of a confident man.

I could have lingered for a while, but he wanted to get going. The heat inside the gallery was making him tired. He had already invited me for Indian food, a little place right around the corner. I'd brought a bottle of champagne. "To celebrate," I said. My husband was getting married.

I know I should say, ex-husband, but that doesn't sound natural. I don't believe in divorce, even if I was the one who left him.

Earlier in the week, I'd gone out and bought a pair of ice skates. It had been a cold, snowless winter, and if I was going to live in this climate, I figured, I should at least be equipped. I bought a pair of black leather figure skates, men's 9's, but

173

when I reached the pond where my husband was meeting me with our ten year old son, I discovered both skates were for the right foot. "Can you believe this?" I said to him, though weirder things have happened.

They wanted me to come to their wedding. In fact his sister had asked specifically if she and her family could stay at my house. "She can stay," I told him, "whether I'm around or not. But I might be in Siena for the *Palio*. Are you going to take a honeymoon this time?"

Suddenly I felt overwhelmed, and walked over to this bridge where water was leaking, forming stalactite shapes. My son skated over and looked up at me, "Are you crying, Mom?"

"No," I lied. "My skates don't fit."

"Do you want me to push you?" He was such a feeling child, and I said yes, and let him push me, though I didn't really want to be shoved across the ice.

My husband offered to let me use his ice skates, and I accepted. We wore the exact same size, but they were hockey skates and didn't have sharp edges. I felt like they could slip out from beneath me. They didn't have those teeth on the front to help you stop, and I didn't want to fall and break something.

The famous artist had age on his mind. He was trying to figure out how old I was by asking me the ages of my children, the year I was pregnant in Paris. I found him very attractive, similar to the looks of my ex-husband actually, and I didn't mind that he was older. I let him order dinner, but he didn't drink, so I'd left the champagne in my car.

I was feeling high anyway, cheerful, alert. I had purposefully tried to look beautiful. This man had been on my mind, even in my dreams. I was amazed that he had responded to my fan note. Now he seemed to be feeling the situation out. He didn't want to fall on ice either.

I told him that I'd had this dream — He was walking through a gallery, an opening full of people, and how he'd waved at me. I was asked to read "the marriage of true minds," then discovered all my clothes were lined with poetry. All I had to do was open up and read. I realized this was quite an invention, for I could even go to the bathroom and read poetry in my underpants. "What do you think it means?" I asked.

"I'm sure I don't know, but it sounds pretty good." He went on to describe the different dishes as he knew them — the dry, clay-baked, tandoori chicken, the juicier, creamed spinach with lamb. I said that I could eat anything, dying for a beer. I was tired of living alone.

I was still very close to my husband, talked to him on the phone at least once a day, but I also got along very well with the woman he was now marrying. We genuinely liked each other. Perhaps I should have minded that she was not at all jealous. She had given me a lambskin cover for my bike seat at Christmas, and I'd given her real turquoise earrings. It would seem odd if I refused to celebrate their marriage, when I was actually glad that she was the one. I'm sure it would be different if I had a partner. I could hobble across the ice, half-gliding, but I'd rather not.

I couldn't tell if this famous man was interested in me. There were moments when his eyes lit up, when my thinking brushed up against his. "I grew up in a home where beauty was essential," I told him. "Every painting, each object — it all becomes part of you. Most people pull away from beauty, don't you think? Because they're afraid they might feel something. Pain for instance. But artists have to enter in a state of dilation."

"Yes," he said, in complete agreement. "Though it's sad, most painters squeeze the juice out of their work. They're afraid of appearing sentimental. It can take courage to make something beautiful," he said. "It's more acceptable these days to get ugly."

Whatever he created at this point in his career would undoubtedly be applauded, but still, I could see he continued wrestling with the medium, trying to make it new. I wasn't sure if I should go to the wedding.

The globed lights had come on all around the pond and our son was skating the periphery. "All our friends would be wondering how I felt, I don't know. I just think it would give you more freedom if I wasn't there." It might also make me very sad.

"Well, you're invited," my husband said, explaining it away. "That was then, and this is now." But everything past still seemed present to me. Even the future was contained in this moment — We just couldn't see the entire panorama, the ribbon that surrounded our lives.

A year ago I saw a psychic who described a tall, married man, older, with glasses and a prominent nose, as if she could actually *see* him. Now I wondered if it was this artist, who fit the description. He was still married, though his wife had left him for a woman less than six months ago.

"It seems that women usually leave men," I said. "Men only leave a marriage if there's something else lined up."

"That's because men associate marriage with the mother," he answered. "And when it's over, believe me, it's almost like death."

I wasn't sure why I felt so comfortable with this man. Most women would feel intimidated, but it seemed like I almost knew him. He was familiar in this unfamiliar way.

"Do you miss her?" I asked.

"Not at all."

I wondered if this was true. Even though I didn't want my husband back in bed with me, I certainly missed something we'd had, a feeling of wholeness, of skating together, arms linked, feet gliding in tandem.

He asked me if he could have his skates back if I was just going to stand there, shivering. "Sure," I said, and wobbled across the frozen grass to the car. His girlfriend had not shown up. She was making chicken soup because our older son was sick. She was better at mothering than I was, and I was grateful that she cared for my children in my absence.

When my husband put on the skates he was suddenly taller. The famous man *was* taller, and I liked his bony looks, his eyes, when he took off his glasses and left a generous tip. "I hope you enjoyed that. Ready to go?"

He had invited me to stay at his loft — "I've got plenty of room," and though I knew I shouldn't impose, my other city friends were either sick or on vacation, and it was true, he had the entire top floor of this building. One half of it was studio space. Enormous new works were up on the walls — they were like a cross between painting and sculpture. Each canvas had a different object pressing from behind, creating a subtle bulge. I wondered if anything would happen.

I knew men liked me in that way, but I hadn't slept with anyone in over seven months. I'd been writing so much it didn't seem to matter. There were always men interested, hanging around, but for some reason, recently, I hadn't been tempted, and felt like something big was approaching my life. At least that's what I told myself.

As soon as we walked into his living space, the telephone rang. He didn't have an answering machine. He wasn't going to have a machine stand in for him, I guess. "That was my friend," he said, after he had spoken. He didn't elaborate so I didn't ask. Maybe his conscience was getting the better of him. "Do you mind if we don't make a fire?" Having a fireplace was a luxury in New York, and he was almost out of wood. He was not making a move to be romantic.

But the huge space needed warming. "Oh can't we?" I begged.

Once it was lit, he admitted how much he enjoyed watching it, how he didn't do enough for pleasure.

I said, "Pleasure is something we must serve," as if she were a goddess and the fire an offering.

My ex-husband once called me *"la femme de ma vie,"* introducing me to a well-known French poet, while his girlfriend was standing right there. It was a slip that slipped by because of the language, but I was flattered, not just the mother of his children.

I wondered if I should tell my husband about the dream I'd had. We were driving together—he was at the wheel, and I was sitting very close to him. I kissed him on the cheek and said, *You can never be replaced*. When I woke up, I found myself sobbing.

The next morning I called home and my youngest son answered, informing me, "Dad's getting married. He bought her a ring." I wondered if he had paid for it himself this time.

I said to my son, "Oh, I'm glad! Aren't you?"

"I don't know," he said, honestly.

And I felt myself falling.

"Do you want a divorce?" I asked the artist.

"I don't like to think of anything ending," he said. His statements seemed to contradict, but I could accept that. He went on about the suicide rate for men after divorce, how they didn't fare well. "Most women are relieved."

"Maybe at first," I answered. "A false euphoria."

"I was always wrapped up in my painting." He seemed disconcerted, as if he didn't have much time, and I wondered if he wanted to work that very evening.

He no longer seemed all fired up, just tired, and even the logs had quickly settled. The loft was chilly and too big. I pulled an Indian blanket up over me, as I lay back on the sofa, while he sat in his chair. He looked as if he had rested there throughout a very long marriage. He yawned, though it was only ten o'clock. He said that he got up early. That he liked to start painting by seven.

"You can shower," he stood up, and showed me the bathroom, got a pillow for the couch. "When you wake," he added, "I'll make you a nice breakfast." He stooped to check the coals. "You're a good fire maker."

"I should be," I answered, "I'm a fire sign."

"Oh, when?" he wanted to know.

"April thirteenth."

"That's *my* birthday." He seemed astounded, as if he owned the date. But I was not so surprised. We were just like that pair of right skates, too similar to be of any use to each other.

"I'm all fire and air. No water anywhere. No earth," I explained, as if I were a female Icarus, flying a bit too high and close to the sun.

He seemed disenchanted, ready for bed. "So is there anything you'd like?" he asked, meaning cider or a magazine.

"I'd like to be *always* in love," I responded.

"Yes," he smiled. "We need that, don't we." He said goodnight then without giving me a hug, and as soon as he closed the door on the far side of the room, I felt an immense loneliness descending.

The fire had almost burned itself out. It was hardly giving off light or heat. I turned off the lamp and sat in the darkness, wide awake. Then I heard him in his bedroom, talking to someone on the phone. I got up and walked closer, listening for a moment. "I don't care if it's been a year, I just want to see you."

I had this terrible feeling that my presence, my company, had made him feel even more desperate.

I sat back down on the sofa in the darkness, as if I had fallen on the slick, black ice, way out in the middle of nowhere. I could feel the sure cold slowly entering my body, but I did not try to move or make a sound.

THE REPLACEMENT

Why Lionel bought the bird was obvious. It was named "Raquet," and littered its squirt and seed all over the floor of its wrought-iron bird palace, on the surrounding newspaper as well—fair game for the baby to play with, or perhaps I should say more accurately, eat.

Parrots can be so wasteful, and this one cracked open its shells and spat them, while the baby appeared in all eagerness. Even just waiting in her highchair, the infant began imitating the parrot's screech, uttering harsh squawks, not out of hunger or pain, but in response to this insistent bird.

Meanwhile, Lionel kept jumping up every ten minutes with a hand-held vacuum machine to catch the scattered bird spray. No one could have any peace.

I believed that the bird was jealous. During the week she had her master all to herself, and he was generous with his caresses. When he held her and scratched, she made these little piggy sounds—a sure sign of animal contentment.

I kept my distance, seeing what it had done to its ladder, devouring most of the wooden rungs. It had already tried to clip the buttons on my coat, which didn't make me feel too comfortable. That curved beak, those prehistoric claws—I had no urge to get passionate beneath its wing, to tickle its molting feathers.

"Do you see how she's turning from red to green?" Lionel pointed out with enthusiasm.

I did on the other hand pick up the baby, who was worthy of a thousand kisses. I had forgotten how luscious that neck meat was, how constant mothering could be. Lionel was a father on weekends.

"Welcome to the Wild Kingdom!" he answered the phone,

and it *was* a kind of jungle playroom atmosphere, with the huge potted ficus, Racquet harping in the background, but then his face suddenly changed.

His wife was wondering about the baby. Had he given her the medicine. The bottle of sticky pink liquid had tipped and spread across the table.

"She's been on that shit for six weeks!"

Lionel took the parrot up into his arms with great tenderness. At least no one could take this bird away from him. He insisted that I just let the baby crawl around the floor, saying I might spoil her, but I picked her up anyway, holding her high — *Fish out of water! Goose in the air!* Kissing both cheeks, singing song after song, mainly to drown out the bird and the drone of the vacuum cleaner.

I knew he was distracting himself from a seven year failure, but he could not ignore the way he felt. She was trying to reduce his visitation rights, moving away to the country.

"Call your lawyer and see what *he* says, you stupid fuck." Anger, a sure sign of attachment.

I could see that he wanted to do well, heating up the baby food in the microwave oven, trying not to smoke in the same room, waking up with his daughter at 5 a.m., dressing her in tights with little red hearts on them. He would be an irreplaceable presence in her life, even if the mother already had a new man. I would only help him to recover. For I could never tolerate living with a bird.

Each night we had to throw this huge tarp over its cage, but in the morning I could hear it pawing its sand tray in a fury, whenever Lionel and I made love.

I felt that the bird would consume him, munching, discarding, and he would feed himself willingly to her. She would come to demand more and more, and he'd delight in her antics. "She needs room not to damage her feathers."

But really the bird would want all of his attention, until

he would blow up, screaming at his wife—"OK! Go ON! TAKE EVERYTHING." And the parrot would rejoice, squawking in the background, making a noise that sounded something like—*ROT, ROT.*

NOW THAT I'M TOTALLY BLIND

So my son has to say to me, "Is this a *blind* date, Mom?"
I have to admit I've never *seen* him before.
"That qualifies," he says, as if wondering when his mother
will learn from experience.

I know all the anticipation is wearying, the amount of time
spent thinking over what might not amount to anything.

First there is the phone call where you try to make a composite picture of everyone else you've ever known who's also
Scottish, polite, aggressive, Yale and well-to-do.

Most women would *grab* at this profile. Been married twice
(at least he tried), seems genuinely involved with his daughters,
on vacation. But there is something over-eager in his voice,
and the picture reads out: too well groomed.

I would rather be fixed up with a bit of a bear, someone
who absent-mindedly licks honey from his hand. He's got a
stumble in his walk because his head is in the clouds and he's
probably drugged on sex or love. A man who is led by some
deep woodsy scent or who is under the spell of inner music.

But this first blind date tells me (I feel a certain chill) how
he loves to climb mountains without carrying extra oxygen.
I imagine he makes love very fast, that he's a competent cook
but his kitchen's immaculate.

I tell my friend who arranged all this how much I appreciate her thinking of me, how it was such a generous gesture.
Or was it. I spend the entire afternoon in preparation torture—
bathing, scrubbing, shaving, plucking, then the hot curling
iron, making up my face, and finally—What to wear.

I decide on a peach-pink silk blouse with an Etruscan colored necklace, brick with sea-green. I choose my tight black
stretch pants, knowing they're inappropriate, for at the end

of our second conversation he had said how much he admired French women, those lovely little skirts they wore.

"I know," I bristled, "such femininity."

His directions, of course, are impeccable. I also arrive right on time, not wanting to stay late, and I'm all jacked up because I've just sold a song and am going to break the first rule of adult blind dating: Don't talk about yourself—Listen to him.

And then the moment of truth when the screen door swings open. Does the face match the vision? Might I be happily surprised? And what happens to that inner picture at this moment of awakening—is it absorbed back into the imagination, like sperm into the bloodstream of a cauterized man?

Now the date can take off, or you receive that sinking feeling. I think he takes a reading of my face and feels the impact of my unfair first impression, for here he's composed this lovely four course dinner, white carnations on the table, pentatonic bell chimes on the CD upstairs.

I had expected him to look like this British intellectual I'd had a crush on in college. I had hoped that my reading over the phone had been wrong, that he would indeed by sloppy-sexy, dressed in well-worn tweeds, but his blue jeans are pressed and he has tassles on his loafers.

It looks like he's about to rent his house, as if everything personal had been put in the attic. I think fondly of my own little nest, how I like a heap of produce, a sink full of flowers. I don't even mind stepping over piles of clean laundry left on the playroom floor, if I'm heading for the piano with a tune in my head—dinner can always wait, and my son understands this.

But this man will grill our steak outside so we don't have to smell it. I sit beside the salad and think—Lordy lord, now I'll have to spend the next four hours telling him my story and listening to his. Depleted, rather than fulfilled.

When he takes me on "the tour" I can't tell which is his

bedroom. He must make his bed before he even gets out of it. I feel ungrateful, judgmental—he is perfectly nice. It is just that he gives me 20/20 vision.

When he says goodbye that evening, there's no moon in the sky, and I nearly trip as he leads me to the car. I'm afraid in the darkness he might try to kiss me, just to refute the fact the evening was a failure. I turn my head as he descends and cry, "You'll have to see my place!" I can't get to sleep that night fast enough.

All my married friends are dying to fix me up, though no one knows a soul. Then my best friend's sister's ex-lover's uncle comes to town and he looks like a possibility. My friend watches my ears perk up when she describes him to me as "Powerfully Built." He also plays the drums and was once a drug addict. This might seem disarming, but it was nothing with needles, and at least he has struggled and progressed.

I keep him on the phone for forty-five minutes our first phone call, saying anything that comes to mind. When he tells me his name and says, "Need I explain myself?" I tell him rather saucily he has to, and when he says that his children are quite large, meaning older, I say, "I'm glad they're not wimps," and we laugh. He invites himself over saying he'd like to see my garden, though he admits he could also use a home-cooked meal.

I want to tell him straight off—I'm not going to mother you. And I'm not one of those women who has multiple orgasms. And I don't like men who try to prove me wrong on this. But of course if you wait a little while in between times and stroke my sides and murmur dangerous things, I'm bound to do anything again.

I imagine being held in his powerful arms, as if I were returning to the cradle, or my grandmother's sofa, to the hands of my sister who used to play with my hair, braiding it then letting it fall.

I put him off for two weeks to let him know I won't be

easy, plus I want us both to savour the days. My friend admits he has no money, and I say, "That's no good," but then the inner optimist takes over—Maybe his band will hit the top forty next week—frugality turned to fruition.

My friend says that time has taken its toll on him, but I like a man who's had experience, for I'm sure he's not the kind who cleans his fingernails daily, or who'll inspect the top of my refrigerator before he sits down, sniffing at the anchovies in the salad. He will eat. And I will take mysterious pleasure in serving him.

He'll look into my eyes as if he knew my past, as if life just began when he pulled in the driveway, carrying a handful of daffodils he just saw up the road—leaving the car in neutral while he dashed to pick a couple—so that their stems are still viscous and dripping. In his other hand, a bottle of mineral water and a new 45 his band cut last weekeend. "I'm impressed," and insist we listen right away since I'm all spun out by this person.

I can feel his physical presence right behind me as I gambol through the house, glancing over my shoulder to catch his eyebrows lifting up. My heart *leaps*—another good indication. I let the music begin and lay the flowers on their side beside the green water bottle. It seems natural that he reaches for my hand, and we start to do a little slow jitter-bug—trying out familiar steps as if we'd shared the same highschool. I like the fact that he's slightly overweight and I'm drawn to his smell. I want to throw back my head and let the good times roll, saying—Haven't we met somewhere before? Maybe in some other lifetime? It seems a confirmation when he pulls me closer to him, wanting to dance cheek to cheek. He whispers, "Close your eyes," and I say to myself—Remember, you are totally blind.

THE ART OF KISSING AT THE AGE OF FORTY

Listen to this," my son says, tilting back in the kitchen chair so I have to swat him — He's trying to break that chair in half. *"The Vacuum Kiss,"* he reads. *"The moment she responds suck inwards as though you were trying to draw out the innards of an orange."*

"My word," I say. Where did Father O'Reilly ever get this book.

I've been getting counsel from Father O'Reilly ever since that drunken bum Dad of theirs wanted these boys back in his life. He wanted to take them to Disney World *this* Good Friday, which happens to be my birthday. "Over my dead body," I said.

Father O'Reilly doesn't say much, but it helps to have him listen. I've been off men completely three years now, and I think it makes me kind of crusty. Sometimes I feel like an alligator mom *hissin'* on her high egg heap. These boys were baked on the warm side.

But what's strange is now I got this feeling for O'Reilly. I tell you I haven't told the worst. It struck me over Mass one Sunday before Lent — He looked so beautiful in his vestments, though he's not considered to be a handsome man. But as soon as the incense passed me, that was it — I saw his private parts swinging beneath his robes, swaying like the Holy Trinity. I immediately put that out of my mind. But once in a while I *see* things, and now this has got me in its grip.

So here I am at the age of forty in the same upstairs on Dauphine Street, squeezin' an' suckin' a fresh boiled bunch of craw the boys brought up for my birthday. They're making a fuss in the sweetest way, keeping me together as usual.

It's a hot night for April and we got the tall windows open both sides of the house. The black lace iron of the balcony stands out against the dirty pink stucco of Lefebre's on the other side of the street. I can hear people partying one block away, though we're out of the center near Ursulines. This town never does seem to quit, and I like it that way, no quitting. Even if we are six feet under sea level and bodies must be buried above. Some things keep floating to the surface.

I've been raising these boys alone ever since their Daddy ran off with the Praline Lady. I swear she even smelled too sweet—tacky, tiny, bleached-blond bitch, and now she's even got him off liquor.

Gaston is twelve. Phillipe about ten. I asked Father O'Reilly if I should tell the older one about you-know-what, wanting to get onto that subject, and he borrowed me this book— *The Art of Kissing*. Must have been written a hundred years ago, but I figured kissing ain't changed much since then.

I wonder if he don't want a woman on occasion, if he ever thinks of me sometimes—what my long hair's like with the braid undone, what my heavy breasts feel like with a summer sweat between them, or does he keep his mind so well swept of all that could be beneath my skirt—brand new pennies and buttered popcorn, fallen magnolia leaves.

Sometimes he makes me so mad I swear—I want to sting him something awful to make him more human, less of a friggin' saint.

"*Every lover is a glutton*," Gaston reads, and Phillipe makes the sound of a pig in heaven, which sends them howling to the floor. They're in the mood for this information, I guess. I decide not to feel irritation, or maybe the rosy wine decides. I might as well enjoy these silly children, though I don't follow up with, "A glutton for punishment," what Mama always said I was.

"Get up you guys, it's my birthday, and I want a proper celebration." I made Gumbo Ya-Ya, big hunks of andouille and a good dark roux, bits of chicken off the bone, pretty hot but not choking. The simmer of it fills the high-ceilinged kitchen, something cozy about this place to me, as if the walls held

190

the yellow smeared history of every biscuit that was beaten here since I was born.

I been sincerely thinking of putting something to O'Reilly, how I'd like to have another child. I've been thinking about a *semination,* maybe the closest I could come to a virgin kind of birth.

I know that my mind has surely wandered, for tonight he'll be doing vespers before the Paschal candle — just a flicker of light in the dark of the cathedral. He might kneel there forever feeling closer and closer to some darkness inside. Loneliness seems to sustain him.

The boys settle down now into savouring, good. They're excited by the Easter parade, already thinking about waking up to find a solid chocolate rabbit with silvery colored eggs. They insist they haven't outgrown the need for it. Only then do they allow themselves to be scrubbed and slicked clean, popped into those white linen jackets Mama made.

Gaston will be taking communion, while Phillipe gets so solemn left behind. I can't ever make the mistake of letting the two of them sit together — They start in hysterical, getting worse when they try to stop.

"Center your lips so when you make contact, there will be a perfect union."

"Yum yum," little Phillipe pretends to woo me, smacking up from his soup. There's something so fresh and sweet about this boy — He's almost like nectar breathing. I see a bud of a religious nature and wish he'd spend more time with Father O'Reilly, but I don't trust my *motifs* on that.

I kiss the air in Phillipe's direction. I love the dark physical feel of these boys. I would never go so far as to kiss them on the lips. My own Mama had that sorry habit, and look at my brother now, Roy. They call him "Le Roi" these days down on Bourbon at that "Boys Will Be Girls" nightclub. I wonder what kind of folks want to see that. I don't even like thinking about his tiny tits or whatever else he's done to himself.

I wonder about those priests though, all celibates like me. Sometimes you see them embracing, and it almost makes me jealous, the kinship they got, as if they had the *vantage* of some higher love, and it makes me feel on the outside, the outside of some "*Unh-Unh* wall," with its jagged sharp bits of broken glass along the top—so I say I don't want it anyway. And pour myself more sweet rosé.

"There should never be a let down in a kissing session," Gaston reads aloud, and I want to agree, though I'm mighty estranged from that subject.

At least these boys were conceived, and their father, when sober, was a merciless lover. I hate the fact that I sometimes still long for it.

Yes I want to pour a little red pepper down Father O'Reilly's ear, mixed in with ground alligator horn. The women in The Quarter, they call this "a potion." He's only tolerant of my feelings for him. His smile is the smile of limitation. He's not afraid to insult my femininity that way. Well he should be afraid, I tell you! Don't he know about those little wax men? I could take a flame to his crotch and go melt it—then we'd see all the things he'd want to do.

But how can I *not* love a man like that, soft and gentle as a good pelt of nutria, softest fur you ever felt, like sinking your hand into a deep pail of ashes. Yet something about his humbleness gets to me. I want to rile up O'Reilly! Or maybe have what he has—that sense that he's found his only partner. Maybe it's the Holy Mother Mary, and how can I be mad at her.

There was talk in The Quarter a while back, about this priest and this nun who had a love affair going, three long years, and when they found out, she was expelled, but they kept him on. Think about that for a minute.

The last time Father O'Reilly asked about the health of my children, I looked at him like he was some loser from hell and said, "Don't worry, we three'll survive."

"Survival is the least of my worries," he said, but then

he seemed to sadden when he said to me, "It's difficult, you know, for me too."

So it starts pouring rain and the air is moist and heated. Some people hate it and love to complain, but I thrive when my skin is pearled with sweat. Uncle Lafe liked to say, "A woman hates to be cold!" Now that might be the smartest thing a man ever said.

I would like to surprise Father O'Reilly with a kiss — come upon him while he's dozing in the afternoon sun, and just barely brush his lips.

Somebody turns off the lights on me — Phillipe's bringing my cake and there are so many candles I'd rather not count. I had told him that four would do, but can you believe it — they made this themselves, Mama's own recipec, powdered sugar over lemon, my favorite.

"Blow out yer candles, Ma!" Phillipe says, placing the shining cake down before me, while Gaston holds a fork to my neck, so's I can't lean any closer.

"Don't I even get to wish?"

OK, they agree, though mothers are too old for wanting wishes, right? Anyway, I'm allowed to close my eyes, while the candles are heating up the lemon — Dear Angel of Sweet Love in Heaven — *one kiss* — then I blow them all out with a puff. Why does this disappoint them.

"Ever since you stopped smoking, Ma."

"I wouldn't mind a picayune right now," I say, remembering a tiny strong cup of coffee with something sweet on the side, or late at night after an hour of deep kissing, both of us a little drunk and perspiration trickling with the music coming up from Audrey's, giving us this endles rhythm. How long it has been since I smoked, since I had a man beside me.

"Why you want a cigarette," Phillipe wants to know.

"To take this lonely feeling out of my chest," I say, though right now I'm happy and they seem to understand this.

"You'll be even more lonely if you smoke.".

Their father is a fiend, a chain-smoker, especially now since he gave up on liquor and moved away. He won't fly in a plane cause of all the No Smoking—that's his reason why he don't come to visit.

The boys together have given me a blue stone brooch. "This is the prettiest thing I ever seen!" They are pleased I'm so pleased, and then a present from Mama, a small cloth purse, padded cotton, homemade.

Phillipe puts his hand inside it. "This could work as a pot holder," he says, and we laugh, cause we *need* a pot holder, unlike those pillows last year—Mama stuffed 'em with blackened Spanish moss.

She lives out by Slidell now, near the Honey Island Swamp. She moved out there to be by Sister when Uncle Lafe died. He was a nutria hunter, softest fur you ever felt. Now I wouldn't mind a pillow made of that!

The boys love the bayou, love the fishing out there, love Mama's fried catfish *beignets*, the silent easy boat life—spider lilies now in bloom, wild iris and wisteria in the bushes. "When we going to the bayou?" demands Gaston.

"Anytime," I say. "Anytime bayou self." They know I prefer the close-in comforts of The Quarter. I think all that silence is for spooks, and keep thinking about the time that cottonmouth dropped right into our boat, smelling for all this world like peeled cucumber.

When Phillipe pulls his hand from Mama's purse, I notice he got the raw red rash on his knuckles. "I bet you got that from your father," I regret to say, meaning the *exma*.

"I got a lot from my Daddy," Phillipe grins. "I'll probably be bald by the time I'm seventeen."

"Surely there is more to your tongue than just the tip of it," Gaston reads.

"Do you mind!" I say. It seems Gaston has gotten to the good part.

194

I do want these boys to be comfortable in their bodies, more than I was allowed at their age. Father O'Reilly doesn't even seem to have a body at times, just these floating testicles. Or maybe his body stops half-way, like those pictures of angels.

But what about me? Isn't he ever tempted to touch my chestnut hair? See how it feels when I wash it with water from the barrel and then comb it out in the sun, spray a little of Aunt Libby's rose water on it, how lush and pretty it feels.

I braid it mostly to get it out of the way. Some people say it's about time to cut it. Was different when their father was around. Most men like real long hair and these breasts.

"Nature kisses in her way but doesn't have the brains to benefit. What's that supposed to mean?" Gaston asks.

"Ask Father O'Reilly, Mama's special friend."

"Don't you dare," I snap, almost rising from the table.

I sought out this book for Gaston after finding a note in his pocket: *If you don't kiss her pretty soon she'll think you don't like her.* What's *that* supposed to mean, I could have asked.

"Is a kiss really a personal salute?" asks Phillipe.

"How should I know, I'm not the army."

"She hasn't been kissed in three years," Gaston says. I feel the impulse to slap him, but burst into tears. They understand that these birthdays make me temperamental. Phillipe pats my back and they are both dead silent. Suddenly I get this picture of being in Father O'Reilly's arms and I look at them both and smile as if ecstatic.

Some women in The Quarter, they say I'm psychic, but I don't want to probe into no future. Let the future come to me. Let him also come, willing, slipping through the dark arcades.

Yes, I think I see his eyes now — they are filling with tears, because he has to part with Mary. And then I understand it's 'cause he's coming to me — out the big doors of the vestry

195

through the garden in moonlight, coming to stand beneath my railing. I am sleeping but I have this dream.

I am sending Phillipe away from me, as if he had to escape, and just before we part he turns his face up and asks, "Mama, aren't you gonna *miss* me?" I am too heart-broken to say, but give him this statue of a golden calf, before I seize him, then send him away from me.

"Linger longer on her lips than you ever lingered before."

"Now that sounds real pretty," I compliment Gaston.

Phillipe is playing with the candle wax, dripping it on his hand. Gaston looks up and says to him, "Don't!" So Phillipe lets it harden and then crumbles it on the table as if he didn't have a mind.

It makes me think of the tight cotton gloves we wore as children, my sisters and I—They fit so snug and had those ridges up the fingers, patent leather pumps and thin socks that slipped down, crinoline skirts, keeping the pink material up, not very modest, we weren't *aimin'* for modest, and Mama used to freshen up our Easter hats with new satin ribbons, a bunch of flowers on the side, fake ones that lasted—We felt like really something coming out of church, and that's when I seemed to be reborn, so happy about the light coming back into the world, like hope, the sweet plumes of smoke going up and the lingering smell of the candles.

Still, I don't want nobody to flash no overheads on now and wake me from this lazy turning over in my mind, as if the sheets were cool clean and our bodies were spooning—I don't care if I am one big fool for wanting a man who only wants to save me.

You know I'd begin very lightly, by removing his glasses, soothing those places where he's tired the most, and he would sit back giving into my breathing for I'd breathe my way slowly around his ear without touching and down along his neck until a shudder ran through him and his mouth sought mine out at long last.

Does he know that tonight it's my birthday? Or is he only thinking about betrayal and death. "A woman can also be forsaken," I once told him.

He said, "Marriages are made in heaven. They can not be undone here on earth."

So now I have to wonder—Will I ever have a partner? And if he doesn't kiss me soon, what are wishes worth.

THE NIGHT BEFORE THE EARTH FROZE

Leave the mother on the rim with the rest of civilization. Coming to the canyon I feel dizzy, overwhelmed. Like dropping into new love, whole worlds begin opening—The climate here surrounds us growing warmer with each step. Geology of red rock deepest inhalation—huge mountains underwater suddenly undrenched. The light at such frequency only flowers can hear it—banging into bloom. All resistance shattered in this playground of the spirits. Love fills forever what death hollows out.

There she is, my Nangiyala, sweet camp at the end. To have died and survived it, born back into spring. The little stone cottages stand under cottonwoods—Angel Bright Creek, glimmering with big fish. Here are my sons. We are waiting for my father who is walking to be with us. Dazed by exhaustion and the even sweeter sun. Wine fills my glass cup. He staggers down the path carrying his box lunch. Fleet smell of wood smoke and the wild mule deer. Life has become immense yet approachable. Love's waiting in the saddle and I'm heading there.

The death of a dog is the end of an era. The night before the earth froze I found her lying in the barn. Dreamt she broke her ice grave and ran up the hill to me. Bouyant, my sun dog, I wrapped her in my arms. Came back to tell you what I couldn't possibly tell you. Can I say what I saw? Having risen to the rim, having tasted the switchbacks of kisses and gingerale, following the one trail of true generosity—to live into abandon (heart in preparation) so that life can come into us, and death can move out.

Patagonia like a drum with mountains breaking out of it. End of pretense, pretending, that I like to be alone. Up upon the mesa the grasses are trembling. Black birds in mesquite sing with raucous sweetness. There's a message by the telephone. The wisteria has begun and there's cotton in the cottonwoods. Hardest to feel helpless. Help us to get over this. Filling up the cavern with pure light and oxygen. To no longer cloak feelings with smoke to not hurt. Sight could crack glass here, melt then remold it—Golden palominos quivering to go.

One must feed the soul as well as the refrigerator. Mathematics says a bumblebee is not supposed to fly. There is the love milk of the mother and there are also cow units. There is sexual fusion and there is also good exercise. Suddenly the gift to us shimmers like birth, solid yet slippery, to be thrown back or kept. There is the paint chip and striation. There are airplanes and angels slipping through eternity, happiness their holiday— Their vocation is to give. One accepts without resistance or deadbolts against it. Two people come together and look over the edge.

I see the end of an era as an opening of arena. Riding without reason for life has gone rodeo. So many, so many saddles to choose from. I'm one with this heavy one his mother used to sit upon. Roll me in your comforter, drink away thirst. To consume and be devoured, so much surface, as if sculpted, his hand moving over me, turned to terrain, gulfing and engulfing, rain in arroyo, I want to take him in my teeth and shake him like a cloth. When he lays back his head his smile fills the canyon. He has made me, unmade me, remade me very happy. All breathing falls to him.

The only phantom here is all we've lost to love. I don't see any losers. End of era. Old and sick, she walked into the barn. I found her at the bottom to the hayloft ladder, stiff and dusty like some rumpled rug. I carried her home to where the stars made their statement — End of marriage, long over. No wheel, only spokes. But the worst was coming home to no merging of welcome. Only a white house, plain yard, the children at their father's. I believe in resurrection. Spirits in the squash bloom. All the rest lies in Tombstone: "Walk where they fell."

Timing is everything. Time took us on her knee and smoothed us with velveteen. Time said — you can trust me, for now you must depart. So I left after midnight, mesa in moonlight, mountains in the distance and occasional dips. I played Oldies but Goodies, sang along a little nervous to be so far away on a singular dirt road. The eroticized motion of *zipping* over cattle guards. "How will I know if you ever make it home?" Now back east a chilly light shines only at periphery, while his voice, a certain presence, still warms me through.

I place myself back in the adobe walled patio, where the hummingbirds zing and zip this p.o. May these words fly into you. May sweetness be your food. May the sunlight in that garden with the statue of Assisi, who could talk with the blackbirds and sing with the dogs, keep our small love protected, human-sized but sacred. I see an earth colored wall next to bright turquoise trim, fuschia colored flowers and my solid yellow cup. All of it delights me as surely as you have done. The sun dog in memory, amidst the fallen golden apples, dozing on her two paws, waiting for return.

THE FINAL SIMPLICITY OF LOVE

I realized tonight as I left your place, that my love for you was absolute. It could go on record with 12 months to the year, 365 days, 7 celestial bodies — Nothing I can do about it. I could tell you more news, that beavers, for instance, have see-through eyelids for swimming underwater, and a tweezer on the tip of the left fourth finger. I would like to be about that useful, but I can also assume the position of a Swiss Army knife in every-ready closed position. I could slap you awake to the presence of my love, like a beaver's tail smacks water, but I want you to be simply as you are, to work in this world as you were meant to do, 24 hours to the day, 52 weeks, and nothing to be done about it. I bask in the inevitable like an eagle in a tuck. Did you know they can dive up to 400 miles per hour? But I certainly wouldn't want to hunt you down. I step back and simply gaze at your true blue shirt and wonder about the immense and awesome wonder of this, not even hoping for an instant that someday you might wake up to the vague possibility, as if turning to an alluring aroma, or hearing the perfect pitch of that one holding note that doesn't die away when your head hits the pillow. It's just a pleasure that I know your name. That it happens to be you. What if I had fallen for some disgusting person. What if I wanted anything in return. Impossible, I know that. My love is simply like a good weather prediction that gets even better when it comes true in my head. Fabulous mild temperatures that inspire you to write the next great chapter. You feel better and even better about yourself, and don't know why. While I'm like a big happy animal, galloping amongst so many shades of green, with heapings of health and sweet frolickings to boot. I want you to be just as you are, 7 days to the week, every 60 seconds, in absolute recurring devotion. Forever and ever as witnessed by the stars, and there's nothing in the world I can do! But to hand you this manuscript and touch you on the mouth, then to blissfully and quietly depart. Don't worry about me. I will be happy as a lark. Pleasure is my mentor, but you can think of me as Joy. I will love you until the day I die. And possibly even after. Read this like my last will and testament, for whatever I have left, I leave it all to you — so lucky I was to have you even barely in my life, which is composed to 41 years now, one month and 16 days, 12 hours and 8 minutes, right up until this very instant — beneath the heavenly, breathing, sky.

Printed November 1991 in Santa Barbara & Ann
Arbor for the Black Sparrow Press by Mackintosh
Typography & Edwards Brothers Inc. Text set in
Baskerville by Words Worth. Design by Barbara Martin.
This edition is published in paper wrappers; there
are 200 hardcover trade copies; 125 hardcover copies
have been numbered & signed by the author; & 26 copies
handbound in boards by Earle Gray have been
lettered & signed by the author.

PHOTO: Lisa Sheble

LAURA CHESTER is the author of over twelve volumes of poetry, fiction and nonfiction. Her most recent books include *Free Rein*, new writing from Burning Deck Press; *Lupus Novice*, an account of her personal struggle and breakthrough with the auto-immune disease S.L.E., Station Hill Press; and *In the Zone: New and Selected Writing*, *The Stone Baby* and *Bitches Ride Alone*, all from Black Sparrow Press. One of the founding editors of the innovative small press The Figures, she went on to edit several important anthologies, *Rising Tides: 20th Century American Women Poets*, Simon & Schuster; *Deep Down: New Sensual Writing by Women; Cradle and All: Women Writers on Pregnancy and Birth*, Faber & Faber; and most recently *The Unmade Bed: Sensual Writing on Married Love*. Presently working on a novel, *The Story of the Lake*, she lives in the Berkshires of Massachusetts.